The Double Cousins
And the Mystery of the Russian Jewels

The Double Cousins
And the Mystery of the Russian Jewels

MIRIAM JONES BRADLEY

AMBASSADOR INTERNATIONAL
GREENVILLE, SOUTH CAROLINA & BELFAST, NORTHERN IRELAND

www.ambassador-international.com

The Double Cousins
And the Mystery of the Russian Jewels

© 2016 by Miriam Jones Bradley

Printed in the United States of America

Library of Congress Control Number: 2016948069

ISBN: 978-1-62020-570-9
eISBN: 978-1-62020-593-8

Cover Design and Page Layout by Hannah Nichols
Ebook Conversion by Anna Riebe Raats

AMBASSADOR INTERNATIONAL
Emerald House
411 University Ridge, Suite B14
Greenville, SC 29601, USA
www.ambassador-international.com

AMBASSADOR BOOKS
The Mount
2 Woodstock Link
Belfast, BT6 8DD, Northern Ireland, UK

The colophon is a trademark of Ambassador

Dedication:

This book is dedicated to the two mothers God gave me. To the memory of Nora Ann McKnight Jones, my mommy who loved me first, and taught me above all to love Jesus. And to my mom, Dortha Onstott Jones who picked up the baton after Mommy went to heaven. She loved us when she didn't have to and she taught me to be a woman of God.

Author's Notes

When I was in kindergarten we moved to North Platte, Nebraska. We lived there until the summer after 8th grade, so when people ask me where I grew up, I say North Platte. Those few years were by-far the most eventful years of my childhood. During that time my mother contracted a virus which destroyed her heart muscle and she went to heaven. I was ten. Then, when I was twelve my daddy remarried and we were blessed with another woman to be our Mom. When I was writing the first Double Cousins book—set on my grandparent's ranch—it was natural to have Carly live in North Platte. After all, that is where we lived when I was Carly's age. That is where we lived when we spent those wonderful weeks at the ranch with our cousins. It is also where I fell in love with books and mysteries.

Since Carly lives in North Platte, I let her live in "my house" and "my neighborhood." I gave her a friend who goes to "my school," Washington Elementary. So, the setting for this book is very familiar to me and very close to my heart. I hope you come to love North Platte as much as I do.

During the time we lived there an arena was built and we attended one of the first re-enactments of Buffalo Bill's Wild West Show. It was a big deal. We visited Buffalo Bill's Rest Ranch several times, climbed Sioux lookout, and had church picnics at Cody Park. I loved the carousel at the park, cotton candy, and the peacocks with their incredible colors.

I wanted to include all of my favorite places in this book, but it had been over forty years since I spent any time in North Platte. I turned to the students at Washington Elementary for help with descriptions of these tourist places and some that were new since I lived there. I would like to thank Mr. Greg Fruhwirth, the principal at Washington Elementary, as well as Diana Woodill and her 2015-2016 fifth grade students Nelia, Gabe, Bennett, Kendra, McKinley, Rayanne, Calvin, Ciara, Ozzy, Jay, Samantha, Branden, and Jacen for the invaluable help they gave me through the descriptions they wrote of the different sites!

As I researched the town I learned more about Buffalo Bill. I read the biography *Last of the Great Scouts*—written by his sister Helen Cody Wetmore—and was impressed with this colorful character. It is true that the Archduke Alexis of Russia visited North Platte and went buffalo hunting with Buffalo Bill. It is also true that he gave some trinkets as souvenirs to Buffalo Bill. There really were Pawnee scouts who were there and were friends with Buffalo Bill. But the details of those souvenirs and the character of Simon are completely figments of my imagination.

In 1973, seemingly overnight, the old depot in North Platte was torn down. There was an uproar. This wasn't just any old building. Not even any old historic building. This depot was the site of the World War Two Canteen which was provided for all of the soldiers who stopped at North Platte for a ten or fifteen minute break on their way across the country. Yes, it was a huge loss. My dad was horrified, and his reaction has stayed with me. I knew I wanted to include the depot in the story. To find out more about the depot and the canteen you can read the book *Once Upon A Town* by Bob Greene.

So, there you have the historic elements that shine in this book. None of the characters in the book are meant to represent real people.

As always, a special thanks to my husband Dr. Bruce Bradley, for his unflagging support. The plot of this book was solidified and developed in the car between North Platte and North Carolina and he is as much responsible for the story as I am.

Thanks also to my wonderful beta readers and editorial readers. I have a group of people who read all of my books and they really help me catch the plot holes and oopsie-daisies of writing! I couldn't do it without you Bruce Bradley, Jessica Cook, Brad and Sarah Calhoun, Phyllis Thomas, Ginny Bradley, and Doug and Jan Bennett and their granddaughter, Katie Blackstock.

Contents

CHAPTER 1

Fort Cody

CARLY WANTED TO LAUGH SO bad her sides hurt. Finally, she lost the battle in a grand snort-laugh. She couldn't help it. Her double cousin Chad stood completely still, just inside the door of Fort Cody, jaw slack, eyes bugged out, head swiveling like a bobble-head doll. Slowly, he raised his arms, reaching out as if to welcome someone.

Max, Chad's ten-year-old brother, poked Carly. "What's so funny?" Carly pointed to Chad and doubled over in laughter. Max grinned. "You said he would like Fort Cody. Guess you're right."

"Where to start, that is the question," Chad muttered. He pulled off the always-present, over-sized, black cowboy hat and scratched his head.

"Watch for it, here he goes," Max said.

Chad blinked, then as if shot like a ball from a cannon, he launched across the room toward the sign that announced, "Buffalo Bill's Wild West."

"And he's off," Max intoned. "To the eight-year-old cowboy wannabe mecca, Fort Cody, in North Platte, Nebraska." His

13

voice rose as he spoke until by the end he sounded like a rodeo announcer.

The ladies behind the counter burst out laughing.

"What did we miss?" asked Kate, Carly's next-door neighbor. Carly's younger sister, Molly, and Aunt Susie appeared beside her. Kate, though a few months younger than ten-year-old Carly, was still a head taller. Hands on her hips, her serious dark eyes searched Carly's face. Her black hair, held back in a ponytail holder, shimmered under the fluorescent lights.

"Must have been something good," Aunt Susie said. "You have the whole place laughing."

"It was all Chad," Carly said. "When he walked in, he was so impressed he couldn't move or talk!"

"Whoa!" Molly said. "Is that even possible?"

The cashier nodded. "We saw it with our own eyes." She winked at the group. "I think he likes it here."

"Max, come take a look at this!" Chad called from the back of the store. "You won't believe it unless you see it!"

"He must have found the two-headed calf," Molly said.

"Two-headed calf?" Max started across the room. "I've got to see that!" He looked over his shoulder. "You coming, Carly?"

"Go ahead. I've seen it." Carly walked over to the counter and smiled at the two ladies. One reminded her of Grandma Johnson with short gray hair, simply cut. She exuded love, and Carly wanted to hug her. The other had bleached blonde spiky hair and a sparkle in her eye. When she moved, Carly caught a whiff of perfume. Not the kind old ladies usually wear, but something that reminded her of a young woman. She looked . . . well . . . spunky and fun. She winked at Carly.

"Have you been here before?" Spike-hair asked.

Carly nodded. "We have, but the boys haven't. Obviously." She looked their way and giggled. Max, down on one knee, examined the stuffed two-headed calf. "They're our cousins and are visiting from South Dakota while their parents and sister are in Washington, D.C. We've told them about this place lots of times. We knew Chad would like coming here, but I wasn't expecting quite that much of a reaction."

Spike-Hair nodded. "I'm glad you brought them by to visit us." She shrugged. "What's not to like? Don't forget to show them the book section." She pointed to the left. "We have the biggest collection of western books anywhere around! The boys already discovered the panorama of Buffalo Bill's Wild West. That in itself is an incredible set. Otherwise, we have all sorts of fun items to look at, and there's a museum in the back. You girls might like the clothing section!"

"My great-grandma Pinky—I called her Gigi Pinky—used to say this is the world's classiest tourist trap," Kate said. She hung her head. "Gigi Pinky brought me here every year for my birthday and let me pick out my own present. My favorite gift was the Native American cloak that's scratchy when I wear it. It has Indian writing on it that reminds me of caveman writing."

"I remember you," the Grandma look-alike said. "You're Pinky Abram's great-granddaughter, aren't you?"

Kate lifted her head. "You knew my Gigi Pinky?"

The lady's face softened. "I sure did. I knew your mother too. They both used to come to the historical society meetings." She clicked her tongue. "We were devastated when your mother passed, and now I'm so sorry Pinky's gone too. What a grand lady!"

A brief smile flashed across Kate's face. "She was something! That's what my dad says."

Carly bit her lip. Her mind rushed back to the day two years ago now when the ambulance screamed up their street and stopped at Kate's house. When it was all over, the doctor said Kate's mother had died instantly from an aneurysm, a burst blood vessel in her brain. That night Carly and Molly huddled on Kate's bed and listened as she told them about it over and over while the adults sat downstairs with her dad and Gigi Pinky. Carly sighed. It was awful, and she knew Kate didn't like to talk about that day very often.

Carly grabbed Kate's arm. "Let's go look at the panorama! I love the Indian village. You can tell Max and Chad the story of your Gigi Pinky's grandpa!"

Kate looked relieved. "Okay. I never get tired of *that* story!"

Spring 1874

Buffalo Bill Cody stood off to the side of the gathering ceremonial group and watched. The chatter of happy voices filled the air. Today was a celebration. Simon, tall and proud in his ceremonial clothes, looked very much like a man ready for marriage. Buffalo Bill fingered the velvet bag in his pocket. It's time, before the ceremony begins. He caught the young Pawnee scout's eye and signaled with his hand. Simon nodded, whispered to the beautiful young lady beside him, and hurried over to his friend and mentor, the famed buffalo hunter and scout.

"So today you make a family," Cody said. He clamped his hand on the young man's shoulder. "You will make a fine husband. It's a privilege to know you."

Simon's eyes flashed with pride and gratitude, and he stood taller. "Thank you. I will miss our work together."

Cody cleared his throat. "Me too, Simon. I understand you must go where you can have land and be with your people, but Oklahoma is so far away."

Simon ducked his head for a moment and then looked the man in the eye. "But for my wife, I must." He shrugged. "Besides, the government has taken our land here. We have nothing."

Cody nodded. "Yes, you must. And, speaking of your bride ... " He pulled the purple velvet bag out of his pocket and held it out. "For you both, a gift from me for your wedding day."

Simon stared. He took the bag. "But there is no need."

Buffalo Bill waved away his arguments. "You earned it. You will see when you open it."

Simon held the gift to his chest with one hand and placed the other hand on Cody's shoulder. "We will treasure this gift, Buffalo Bill. Whenever we look at it, we will remember you. We will tell this story to our children and our children's children." He nodded to Cody, turned and hurried to his bride.

As he stepped back, the old scout could see their heads bowed over the items in the young man's hand. The young lady, barely more than a girl, peeked out from under her eyelashes at Buffalo Bill. She put her hand over her heart, then reached out toward him in a gesture of thanks. He tipped his hat, walked to his horse, sat down and watched as Simon put the lovely necklace on his bride.

"Are you really and truly a Pawnee Indian?" Chad stared at Kate.

"Well, partly. My dad's Swedish. But my mom was part German, part Jew, part Sioux, and the rest Pawnee. The Pawnee were the main Native Americans around here."

"Wow!" Chad pointed to the Native American village in the panorama. "Look at that teepee! I want to live in one of those."

Kate shook her head. "I used to think it would be fun too! But, it wouldn't be very clean. No running water. No toilet, not even an outhouse." She wrinkled up her nose. "Outhouses stink. I kinda like my toilet and shower."

"Me too," Molly said.

"Tell them about your Gigi Pinky's grandpa and Buffalo Bill!" Carly watched Chad for his reaction. She wasn't disappointed. His face flushed, and his eyes sparkled. Even his red hair seemed to glow!

"Buffalo Bill? I'm doing a report for school on Buffalo Bill! Did your family know Buffalo Bill?" Chad bounced from one foot to another.

Kate laughed. "They sure did. Gigi's Grandpa Simon was a Pawnee scout with Buffalo Bill. Gigi Pinky said they became good friends. When the Grand Duke Alexis came to America from Russia, Buffalo Bill took him on a buffalo hunt for his twenty-second birthday. Simon was one of the guides who went along."

Chad was speechless again.

"Tell them about the coins," Molly said. Her eyes twinkled.

"Well, the archduke gave Buffalo Bill some Russian coins as souvenirs. Buffalo Bill liked Simon so well, he gave him two of them. They were passed down through my family. One is over at Gigi Pinky's. She kept it in a special case with the letter Buffalo Bill gave Simon. Her sister Pepper had the other one, but when she died, I guess her daughter got it. I suppose Shelly has it now that her mother has dementia." Kate rattled on like she had told this story a hundred times. "Shelly's my mom's cousin. When they were little their grandmas, Pinky and Pepper, used to take them on trips, but I haven't met her in person. She's like a fashionista or something and travels all over the world going to fashion shows to buy clothes for big stores."

"Back to the buffalo hunt," Max said. "Did they get any buffalo?"

"Oh, yes." Kate tugged on her ponytail. "Buffalo Bill always got buffalo when he hunted. There was also a war dance demonstration by a tribe of Sioux Indians. I had Sioux ancestors there too, I guess. But I'm not sure about that part." She bit her lip. "Gigi Pinky said she didn't know all the connections." Her shoulders drooped. "I miss her. Since mom died, I spent a lot of time with her, especially while Dad's at work. I went to her apartment every day after school."

"She lived in an apartment above Kate's dad's office downtown," Carly explained to Max and Chad. "She lived there a long time, didn't she?" Carly asked Kate.

Kate rolled her eyes. "Long enough that the place is jam-packed with stuff. She never threw anything away. Letters. Newspaper articles. Anything she was interested in is all there, drowning in pink."

"Pink?" Chad wrinkled his nose. "How can you drown in a color?"

"You'll just have to see for yourself, I guess. Why do you think she was called *Pinky?*" Kate giggled. "Her real name was Myrtle, and Aunt Pepper's name was Mabel. Daddy says we have to get the apartment cleaned out so we can rent it, but he can't stand going up there with all the pink. He says it numbs his brain!"

Nine-year-old Molly giggled. "Can't you just throw the stuff out?"

"No!" Kate exclaimed, horrified. "There are some valuable documents mixed in. Historic records, letters from my mother, plus the family heirloom, the Russian necklace that Buffalo Bill gave Simon for his bride." Kate ticked the items off using her fingers. "Who knows what else?" She shrugged. "Daddy says there's probably money or stocks and bonds, whatever those are." She threw her hands in the air. "Anyway, we have to sort through all of it, and that takes time."

Aunt Susie put her arm around Kate. "I'd be happy to help. I met Pinky only once, but she was my kind of gal. I'd love to get to know her better through the things she saved."

An amazing idea shot into Carly's mind. "Why don't we all help? We have a whole week of spring break. We should be able to get a lot done!"

"Would you?" Kate's face brightened, then just as quickly sobered. "You don't want to spend your whole break in that apartment, though."

"Well, not the whole time," Carly admitted. She could see Max giving her "the look." The one that meant, *Are you crazy?* Carly stuck out her chin. "Anyway, it would be fun. And we might learn more about Buffalo Bill." Carly looked sideways at Chad. That should get *him* to agree. Then Max would be outnumbered.

"I'll help," Chad said. "I don't care about the necklace, but I want to see that coin."

Max sighed. "All right, I'm in. But not all day, every day."

Half an hour later, after examining every part of the extensive diorama and looking through the book and souvenir sections, Max finally dragged Chad out the door. "I'll be back," Chad promised the ladies at the counter as he paid for the Buffalo Bill book. "My cousin Slim will bring me." A grin spread across his face. "We didn't know he was our cousin until last summer when we met him at Grandpa's ranch and figured out the mystery of the missing watch. He lives here now, in an apartment behind Molly's house. He's at college today or he would be with us. One day I'll get him to bring me back here."

Max tugged on his brother's arm. "C'mon, Chad. These ladies don't want to hear all of that." *Just once I'd like to get out of a place without Chad spilling all of our business.* "Besides," he said, "we have to go to Kate's dad's office downtown to talk to him about helping with her Gigi's apartment. It could be interesting." A glimmer of hope bounced through Max's mind. *Maybe he won't want a bunch of kids going through her stuff.*

Chad shuffled across the parking lot, scraping his feet on the asphalt. Max felt his neck tighten. Chad knew that drove him nuts. "Hurry up, Chad. They're waiting on us."

Chad walked faster, but still shuffled. "You said cleaning out that lady's stuff should be interesting, but your voice doesn't sound like you think that's true."

Max shook his head. "Well, let's just say I didn't think we would spend spring break looking through an old lady's things."

"You're jealous of Kate, aren't you?" Chad stopped and looked up at Max.

Max swallowed hard. *Where on earth does he get these ideas?* "Don't say that! But she is eating up a lot of our time, and Carly spends all of her time—" He stopped. "Never mind."

Chad jerked his arm away. "It's not like she has any sisters or brothers. She doesn't even have a mom."

Max sighed. He knew Chad was right. But he had looked forward all winter to spring break and spending time with Carly, and now Kate was going to fill all of their time with her project.

He opened the car door, shoved his brother in, and climbed into the seat after him. *This is going to be the worst spring break ever.*

CHAPTER 2

PINK!

AT THE OFFICE THEY HAD to wait a few minutes since Kate's dad, an optometrist, was with a patient. Chad and Max both filled little paper cups with water from the water machine, but Carly wasn't thirsty. She sat between Molly and Kate and looked at the TV monitor while a pretty lady described the different foods that help keep your vision strong. Carly wasn't listening, though.

What's wrong with Max? I thought he would want to help. Carly bit her lip and looked sideways at Kate, who sat eyes forward, no expression on her face. *Daddy called it her stoic face. What if Max and Kate don't get along? I don't want her mad at me; after all, she is my best non-family friend, and she practically lives at our house. But I can't let anything come between me and Max.* Carly looked over at him. He leaned back in his seat, hands behind his head, and stared at the ceiling. She tried to send a nonverbal message, but his eyes seemed to be boring a hole right through the roof. "Max, what are you looking at?"

Max jumped. "I was counting the bumps on that ceiling tile." He grimaced. "I was imagining the extent of the pinkness."

A tiny smile crossed Kate's face. "It's extreme, Max. Might scare you right out of the building, and you'll decide you don't want anything to do with Gigi Pinky's stuff. I wouldn't blame you." She leaned forward and looked right at Max. "I don't want to ruin your spring break."

Max squirmed in his seat. "Oh, it's okay. I don't mind helping," he mumbled.

"Wait until you see it before you decide."

Carly jumped at the sound of a man's voice. Kate's dad, wearing a white lab coat over khaki pants, a striped shirt, and a tie, stood in the doorway. "I hear you kids and your aunt think you want to help sort Pinky's things." He shook his head. "So much pink." He sat down in the chair next to Max. "The thing is, my wife told me several times that when Pinky passed, we would have a chore. 'We can't simply throw things out,' she would say, 'because Pinky's a stasher.'"

"A stasher?" Max asked. "What's that?"

"Exactly what I asked her! She said it's someone who stashes important belongings in unimportant places. I think Kathy made the word up herself. She said we were likely to find important or valuable items tucked in between a couple of old letters. She fully expected to uncover a mystery when her grandma died. Plus, there's the matter of that heirloom necklace. I know the family's very concerned about where Pinky put it." He rubbed his forehead. "Sure wish Kathy was here to handle all of this."

"A mystery?" Max sat up straighter.

Dr. Nate blinked. "Hey, are you the cousins who always get into mysteries with Carly and Molly?"

Max grinned. "I guess that's one way to put it. If there's a mystery to be found, we seem to find it, or it seems to find us." He stuck his hand out. "I'm Max Rawson." He pointed to Chad. "That's my brother Chad."

Dr. Nate grinned. "Love the hat, Chad." He stood up and waved an arm. "Follow me, kids. I think we might be able to find you a mystery, or at least an adventure."

The children jumped up and hurried after Dr. Nate. Aunt Susie brought up the rear. Dr. Nate led them through the office rooms where the smell of clean ruled, then into a storage area. "These rooms back here can be kind of confusing. We have so many doors into various areas; you can almost get lost!" At the back wall he veered left, and Carly saw a staircase leading upstairs. On the right was a metal door. "That door goes into the alley, and it's the exit for the apartment. We tried and tried to get Pinky to move out of here, but she wouldn't have anything to do with the idea." He pointed to the chair lift hooked to the rail on the right side of the stairs. "That was our compromise. We had this put in so she could get up and down. She absolutely refused to leave her little home, and you know, when she said no, it was useless to try to convince her otherwise."

Carly followed Max and Dr. Nate up the stairs. The dark brown rail felt slick from years of polish. The carpet on the steps was worn clear down to the boards in several places. The steps creaked and groaned as she climbed the stairs. The window at the top of the stairs didn't let in much light since it was made of those glass blocks you can't see through. The stairway smelled of old wood, polish, and age.

Once at the top, Carly followed Max through the door into the apartment kitchen and stopped dead in her tracks. The walls were pink. The light fixtures were pink. The tile floor was pink. The cabinets and countertops were pink. The mixer was pink. Even the refrigerator was pink. The others crowded in behind Carly, but no one made a sound.

Finally, Chad choked out the words Carly knew they all were thinking: "It's *so* pink."

Chad turned around and around, chanting:

"Pink! Pink! Pink! Everything is pink!

It doesn't go away, even when I blink.

There's so much pink, it makes my brain shrink.

It overwhelms me till I can't even think!

This much pink could make a ship sink!

Pink, pink, pink, there's too much pink!"

Everyone burst into laughter, but Dr. Nate laughed until he cried. He pulled out a huge white handkerchief and mopped his face. "Oh, Chad. That's exactly how I feel. Wait until you see the bathroom."

Chad shook his head. "I don't know if I can take more pinkness. Is every room this pink?"

Kate shook her head. "No, the furniture in the living room isn't, so that helps a little."

Carly followed Kate around the house. *This will be a lot of work!* Every flat surface was covered by perfectly organized stacks of small boxes. Dozens of photo albums, rows and rows of books, and what looked like journals packed the bookshelves. Picture frames, many containing newspaper articles, crowded the walls. One caught Carly's eye. *Historic North Platte Depot Demolished.* She looked at the picture, and commented, "My daddy told me about this. He said a lot of locals were upset when they tore down the depot."

Dr. Nate shook his head. "It was a tragic mistake on the part of the railroad. All they saw was an old building without a purpose. They didn't think about the historic significance of the World War II canteen. Pinky was livid when they destroyed it in 1973. She and her sister, Pepper, both volunteered at the canteen every Saturday during the war."

"What canteen?" Max asked.

"During the war, locals had a canteen at the depot every day. Trains of soldiers came through here, one after another," Dr. Nate said. "They would stop for ten or fifteen minutes to take on water and coal for the steam engines, and the men would climb off. When they did, they found a group of people ready to serve up sandwiches, cake, hot coffee, and milk—all for free. They could take free cigarettes and magazines too. The local communities banded together and did this for the entire war. They met every train, serving as many as a thousand soldiers a day! Men all over the country still talk about their stop here at the canteen."

"Wow! I had no idea," Max said. "That building would have made a neat museum."

"Sure would have," Aunt Susie said. "There is a depot display at the historic museum by Buffalo Bill's ranch, but it can't take the place of the actual building. Maybe we can visit there later this week!"

"Oh, let's," Molly said. "We've never been."

Aunt Susie nodded and looked around. "Well, despite the pinkness, I'm still excited about this project. I think Pinky must have been quite the lady, and I would love to help."

Max nodded. "Me too. I didn't want to help at first, but who knows, we might find a mystery! We'll have to ask Carly's parents, but if they say it's okay and if you'll let us, Dr. Nate, we would like to help."

Kate grabbed Carly and gave her a big hug. "Oh, thank you. Thank you! This job will be so much more fun with all of you here to help. I'll tell you more Gigi Pinky stories too!"

"When do you want us to start?" Aunt Susie asked. "Would Monday morning work? We have church tomorrow."

"Monday would be great," Dr. Nate said. "We'll get boxes for sorting and packing. Just watch for money, important papers, and a gold and pearl necklace."

Carly nodded. "We'll be careful! We can start with her clothes and dishes. That will clear out some of it."

Dr. Nate nodded. "You have no idea how much that will help. Now, I hear you all wanted to take a look at the Russian coin. You ready to see it before you leave?"

Chad bounced up and down. "I thought we would never get to that part."

Dr. Nate laughed. "Well then, come through the living room. She mounted it in a plastic case and hung it on the wall."

Chad held up his hands. "Wait a minute," he said. "It's not pink, is it?"

Spring 1942, North Platte, Nebraska

Twenty-year-old Myrtle Zimmerman, known by her family and friends as Pinky, waited by the train tracks on a warm spring morning. The breeze lifted her hair and tickled her neck. The smell of cinnamon rose from the covered basket she held in her hands. A thrill ran through her as the faint whistle of a train drifted across North Platte. Pinky grabbed her sister's arm. "Here comes the next train, Pepper."

Pinky and Pepper, just thirteen months apart in age, did nearly everything together, including moving across the state to North Platte for jobs. This Saturday found them in the same place they had been every Saturday since Christmas, when they had come to meet the troops with friends. Pinky's mind flew back to that first unforgettable, frigid day.

The sisters had been working in North Platte for several months, but still the cost of traveling clear home to eastern Nebraska for Christmas was too much. Besides, Pinky had to work the day after Christmas at the bank, and Pepper had to be back at her job in the railroad office the same day. Instead of sitting in their little apartment feeling sorry for themselves, they decided to greet some soldiers. Someone had heard that some of their local National Guard troops would be coming through town on a troop train, so they had organized a party to meet them with gifts and food. Only it wasn't their boys, but soldiers from Kansas.

A smile slipped its way onto Pinky's face when she remembered that day. Wow! The townspeople were disappointed when they realized these weren't their boys, but they decided to give the gifts anyway. The soldiers who arrived were confused at first when complete strangers came on the train and handed out food and gifts. Their gratitude inspired the community, though, and the depot canteen was born.

And now, Pinky couldn't think of anything she would rather do on a Saturday morning. After all, what could be more fun than meeting one thousand handsome soldiers? The whistle blew and the train swept into the station. "Here we go. Let's raise some morale!" she shouted in her sister's ear.

CHAPTER 3

Addicted to Pink

"I'M HUNGRY. MY STOMACH'S GROWLING." Carly rubbed her stomach. "What about you, Molly?" She looked at her sister sitting beside her in the car. "Seems like forever since breakfast."

"It's noon," Molly said. "Mom will have lunch ready, I bet."

Aunt Susie pulled up to the curb at Carly and Molly's home. "Here we are at the corner of 5th and Magnolia. How's that for front door service?"

"Aren't you coming in?" Max unbuckled his seat belt and opened the door.

"I guess I should." Aunt Susie put the car in park and unfastened her belt too. "I can help you explain our big project to Carly's parents."

Carly breathed a sigh of relief. "Oh, good. If they know you'll be there, they will probably let us do it."

"I'll beat you all to the house," Chad said. He dove out of the car and raced toward the front door, the rest of the cousins right behind him.

Carly dashed up the stairs onto the wrap-around porch and stopped short. Chad held the screen door open while he pushed the old fashioned doorbell. To Carly, it sounded like the old alarm clock in the upstairs bedroom at the ranch.

"You don't have to ring it, Chad." Carly reached around him and opened the door. "Just go right in."

"I know," Chad said. "But I like that sound. It sounds like a sick bird."

Carly slipped past him into the house. "Hi, Mom, we're home," she called. She pulled her windbreaker off and hung it on the coat tree behind the front door.

"I kind of got that idea," her mom called from the back of the house. "I'm in the kitchen." Carly made a beeline for the kitchen. "Mmm. Smells good in here! Can I help?"

"Yes, you can set the table and carry things out to the dining room."

Aunt Susie appeared in the doorway, followed closely by the other kids. "Do you have room for one more person at the table?" she asked.

"There's always room for one more," Carly's mom said.

Within five minutes the food was on the table, and they had all washed up and seated themselves at the large dining room table. Max looked around the room while he waited for Uncle Jeff to say grace. *I wish our house was old like this one. These thirteen-foot ceilings are so cool. Tall people wouldn't feel squished in this house.*

The sun filtered through lacy curtains on the bay window and left dainty patterns on the table. They reminded Max of his mom and his older sister, Dorie. They both loved this room, especially the built-in shelves along the wall. *Mom would fill it with knickknacks like Aunt Sheila, though. I'd put books and pictures and sports equipment up there.*

The smell of cheesy potato soup in the bowl in front of him made his stomach growl.

"Let's pray," Uncle Jeff said.

Max bowed his head and thought of his parents and Dorie. Today they would fly to Washington, D.C. Dorie had won the South Dakota state spelling bee, something he still couldn't believe. But because of that, she got a free trip to the nation's capital for the national bee. Mom and Dad were both going with her, and they planned to spend a few days touring the capital city before the bee. Dorie had been so excited about the trip; she had nearly driven Max crazy, between helping her study and hearing about all of the sites they would visit. *I'm glad she's not here this week. We won't have to put up with her bossiness.* His stomach felt hollow. *Sure will be weird, though. I don't think I've ever been here without Dorie.*

"Amen." Uncle Jeff ended his prayer. "What time do your parents and Dorie fly out today?" he asked.

Max jerked his head up. "Um, this afternoon. Four something."

"Four thirty-one," Chad said. "It's four thirty-one."

"Wow! How did you remember that?" Molly asked.

Chad shrugged. "Do you know Kate's great-grandma was addicted to pink?" He scooped a spoonful of cheese soup into his mouth and looked at his uncle, waiting for a response.

"Addicted to pink?" Uncle Jeff raised his eyebrows. "What do you mean?"

Molly giggled. "I think he's right. We went to her apartment today above Dr. Nate's office, and everything is pink. EVERY THING!"

"Are you sure you aren't exaggerating?" Aunt Sheila asked.

Max took a tuna sandwich and passed the plate to Carly. "I would say 90% of everything in that apartment is pink. Even the refrigerator's pink."

Uncle Jeff blinked and shook his head. "Guess that's why they called her Pinky. So, why did you go there?"

The kids all looked at Aunt Susie. She put her spoon down and laughed. "I'm elected, huh? Well, Dr. Nate and Kate need some help. They have to clean out Pinky's apartment, but she was a hoarder—"

"Not a hoarder," Molly said. "A stasher. She stashed important stuff in with everyday things."

"It's a fine line. I'm not sure I can see the difference," Aunt Susie said. "Anyway, we offered to help. I've got a week off before I have to start working on my next book. I want to spend time with the kids, and this would be an opportunity for us to help others."

"You kids really want to spend your spring break in an old lady's apartment?" Uncle Jeff leaned back and pinned Max to his chair with his eyes. Max squirmed. *How on earth does Uncle Jeff do it? He seems to be reading my mind.*

"I wasn't too thrilled at first," he admitted. "But, there's the chance we might find something exciting. Kate's mom thought there could be something mysterious hidden in that apartment."

Uncle Jeff leaned forward and nodded. "Uh-huh. I knew the word *mystery* was bound to appear. But what if you start and it gets boring? Or there's no mystery at all? You know, if you start, you have to finish."

Max looked at Carly. He hadn't thought of that, and he could tell she hadn't either.

"It will be a lot of work, and some of it won't be fun," Carly admitted. "But they need help. There are lots and lots of letters and papers to sort through, and the Russian necklace to find."

"All drowning in pink." Chad held his bowl up. "Can I have more soup?"

Carly took Chad's bowl. "I'll get it. I want some too." She took both bowls and hurried out to the kitchen.

"Russian necklace?" Aunt Sheila said. "Why does she have Russian things? Wasn't Pinky Native American?"

"Yes, she was Pawnee and Sioux, I think," Carly called from the kitchen.

"But Buffalo Bill got them from some grand duke guy when he came here, and then he gave some of the stuff to Kate's ancestor, Simon," Max said.

"The Grand Duke of Russia?" Uncle Jeff scratched his head. "That was Grand Duke Alexis. He came here for a buffalo hunt. It was out by Fort McPherson, outside of Maxwell."

"That's it!" Chad held the spoon in his fist and tapped the table.

Max held his breath as Carly carried the bowls back to the table. *If she spills any, it will burn her!* He watched as she carefully slid one bowl in front of Chad.

"Thanks, Carly. This soup is yummy." Chad blew on the hot soup. "I'll write about the grand duke in my report on Buffalo Bill." He took a spoonful and swallowed. "When does Slim get home? What class did he have today? How long will it take him to learn to manage property? I'm glad he's here." He stopped for a breath and looked surprised when the others laughed.

"Chad, you keep changing the subject," Max said. He shook his head.

Uncle Jeff laughed. "Well, to answer your questions, I don't think Slim will be home until late afternoon; he was going to the homeless shelter after class to volunteer. I don't know which class he had today, but his degree in property management should take two years." He looked at Chad. "There, does that answer your questions?"

Chad nodded. "I'll go see him after he gets home and tell him all about 'Her Pinkness.' Then I can ask him what class he had and if he'll take me back to Fort Cody." His eyes sparkled. "That was the coolest place I've ever been. I could live there. Well . . . " He paused and stared at his soup. "I didn't see any food there, did you?" His forehead wrinkled. "I guess I'd have to have someone bring me food!"

Max looked at Carly and shook his head. "Oh, Chad."

Uncle Jeff chuckled. "Back to the topic at hand. I don't see a problem with you helping the Neilsons. I'm sure they will appreciate it, but if you start, you can't quit. You're committed."

"I think you should spend mornings over there," Aunt Sheila said, "and then pick out some sites you hope to see this week, and we can work them in during the afternoons. You'll have to be diligent to get up and get your chores done first thing in the mornings, but that way you'll have some fun too!"

Max whooped. "Awesome! Thanks!"

"I want to go to the museum out by Buffalo Bill's home," Carly said. "I want to see the depot display."

Her mom nodded. "Great idea, Carly. You know where we keep the packet of tourist pamphlets in the office. Look through them this afternoon and pick the ones you want to see. Remember to look at cost too. Some places charge."

Aunt Susie picked up her plate. "If we're done here, I'll help wash up. Then I better go. I need to clean my house this afternoon."

"Don't worry about the dishes, Susie," her brother said. "These kids can do them."

Carly jumped up. "Let's get them done so we can start planning our week!"

CHAPTER 4

What's the Chance? Slim to Nunn!

AFTER THE COUSINS FINISHED CLEANING the kitchen, Carly ducked into the office and grabbed the folder of bright-colored pamphlets they had picked up at the visitor's center. She snagged several M&M's from the dish on her dad's desk and popped them in her mouth before heading out the door, into the hall, and up the stairs.

Carly loved the upstairs because it was mostly a kid zone. As she climbed the staircase, she glanced as usual out the windows that overlooked the backyard and the small garage. At the top of the stairs, she entered the family room with its huge couch and gas fireplace. Some mornings, Carly came out to find Molly sleeping on the couch, all rolled up in her favorite blanket. The family spent a lot of time up here, especially in the winter when they lounged in front of the crackling fireplace to read or watch a movie. The rest of the time, though, Carly and Molly felt like they had their own living room. Off to the right of the family room was Molly's bedroom, and at the front of the house, Carly's room huddled under the dormer eaves. She loved the cozy feeling she got every time she walked into her room, almost like the ceiling reached down to hug her. This week, Molly had given up her room with its bunk beds to Max and Chad, and she was sleeping in Carly's room. In between the bedrooms was a bathroom; and across the hall, under the eaves, a small play room. Carly called it the library because their parents gave them a bookshelf for Christmas. It was already full.

When Carly got upstairs, she found the other three cousins sprawled across the massive L-shaped couch. Chad's nose was buried in his new Buffalo Bill book, and Molly read the book she had bought at the fort. Max, arms behind his head, sat up when Carly came in. She plopped down on the couch. "Here. There's a pile!"

Chad and Molly put their books down. Carly handed them each some pamphlets. With all of them looking, it didn't take long to pick. Some were definitely summer activities, like the water park. Carly shivered at the thought of swimming now.

"I have to visit Buffalo Bill's ranch," Chad said. He jumped off the couch, book in hand, and bounced from one foot to another in front of the couch.

Max nodded. "Me too! It sounds cool."

"It's an awesome place," Carly said. "I think it looks like a palace. There's no other building around here like it, that's for sure! And the barn is incredible."

In the end they decided on the Buffalo Bill ranch, the museum with the depot display, Cody Park if they could go on a nice day, and the Children's Museum.

"I sure would like to go to the Golden Spike railroad tower," Max said. "But that costs more."

"Let's add it to our list," Carly said. She wrote *Golden Spike* on the list she had started. "I wish Dorie was here. She always wrote stuff down for us."

Max shook his head. "I'm kind of glad she isn't." He grinned. "She won't hassle me about 'growing up' every time I turn around. Besides, you wouldn't believe how excited she was to go on her trip."

"I would be," Molly said. "Is she nervous about the spelling bee? I would be scared to death. I'd probably faint or something."

"A little bit, I guess, but when she gets up to spell, it's like everything else goes away. I don't even think she sees the people in the audience," Max said. "She's pretty tough."

Carly could hear the admiration in Max's voice. *For all his talk, Max really does think Dorie's cool.* "Well, I miss her," Carly said. "And Brandon. I hope he gets to come this weekend."

Eleven-year-old Brandon, another cousin, lived on a ranch a couple hours from North Platte.

"Me too," Max said. "It's not right without him here. Uncle Brad said they'll come Friday evening."

Chad, now standing like a sentry at the back window, shouted. "He's home! Slim's home. But . . . he's not alone."

Carly hurried to the window. She caught a glimpse of a bald-headed man following Slim into the efficiency apartment at the back of the yard. "I don't recognize him. Must be a friend. Maybe someone he met at school."

"Let's go find out." Chad leaped down the top flight of stairs onto the small landing before dashing down the rest of the steps.

"Chad, wait!" Carly raced after him. They weren't supposed to bother Slim. That was one of the rules that went with Slim living in the backyard.

Max and Molly were right behind Carly as she rumbled down the stairs. The three rounded the corner in the kitchen and found Chad slumped dejectedly in the doorway to the back porch. Carly bit her lip. Mom had him by the shoulders. She could tell some explaining was going on. "Let's go back upstairs," Carly muttered.

"You can stay here," Mom called out to them. "Chad just forgot the rule in his excitement. But, don't worry. Slim called, and after supper he'll bring his friend over to meet us."

Max put his fork down and leaned back in the chair. He patted his stomach and let out a huge sigh. "I'm stuffed! That. Was. Good! I love hamburger hot dish. That's why I learned how to make it!"

Carly's mom smiled. "Yes, thank you, Max and Carly, for cooking tonight. You sure made my afternoon easier! I graded a lot of English papers." She stretched. "I still have a pile, but at least I made a good start." Aunt Sheila taught junior high and high school English at the private school Carly and Molly attended.

Uncle Jeff pushed his plate back. "I wanted to tell you a bit about Slim's friend before he comes over."

Max sat up straighter. *What's up now?* He looked over at Carly, but she shrugged.

"Slim's friend's name is Earl. I don't know his last name yet. Slim ran into him at the homeless shelter. They have known each other for almost fifteen years and used to travel together quite a bit."

"He's a train-jumper?" Chad asked. "Does he still ride the rails?"

"Yes and no. He used to, but now he has an old pickup, although it's pretty dilapidated." Uncle Jeff held his hand up as Chad opened his mouth. "I'm not answering a bunch of questions that aren't any of our business. I wanted to let you know ahead of time because I get the idea Earl's kind of shy, and Slim really wants him to stay around so he can help him get his life on track. I thought if you knew some of the facts before they come, it might ease the situation a bit."

Max nodded. "So don't ask a bunch of questions, Chad. Just treat him like he's another friend."

Chad stuck his chin out. "But asking questions is what I do with friends! And I don't ask too many questions. There's just bunches of stuff I want to know. How can I learn stuff if I don't ask? Tell me that!"

Aunt Sheila put her hand on Chad's shoulder. "There's nothing wrong with asking questions, Chad. But sometimes you have to make sure your timing's right. We'd rather have you ask us your questions than to make Earl uncomfortable right off the bat."

The frown eased from Chad's face. "I get it. I'll be polite and not badger him with questions." He shook his head. "But it won't be easy!"

"Hey, how are my favorite eight-to-ten-year-olds?" Slim grabbed Chad and lifted him up onto his shoulders. Chad reached for the ceiling, but there was no way he could reach it in this house. *Neat-o.*

From the vantage point of Slim's shoulders, Chad gave Earl a once-over. *They said I couldn't ask questions, but they didn't say not to look.* The man, his head completely bald, kept his hands stuffed in the pockets of his jeans and his eyes on the floor. He wore a blue plaid flannel shirt. He kind of reminded Chad of Slim the first time they met at the ranch, only this guy was even quieter. Chad's mind flew back to last summer when they first met Slim. They had no idea then that he was their fourth cousin. Chad didn't care what kind of cousin he was. He was just glad Slim was family.

An idea popped into Chad's head. *Hey, it might work! I wouldn't be asking a question, and Mom says it's the polite way to get to know someone 'cause after you talk, the other person is supposed to recipitate, or something like that. And they told me to be polite.* Holding on to Slim's head with his left hand, he leaned over and stuck his right hand out. "Hi, Mr. Earl. I'm Chadwick Rawson, but my friends call me Chad. I'm eight and I want to be a scout like Buffalo Bill Cody when I grow up."

Earl looked up, appearing startled by the burst of words raining down from above. He pulled one hand out of his pocket and shook Chad's hand. "Pleased to meet you, Chad. I'm Paul Earl Nunn, but my friends call me Earl. I read a book about Buffalo Bill when I was a kid. He was somethin'."

His voice was deep, deeper than any Chad had ever heard. Earl's face softened a bit, and he cleared his throat.

Chad sat bolt upright on Slim's shoulder. "Hey, it worked. You recipitated!"

Uncle Jeff laughed. "The word is reciprocate, Chad." He turned to Earl. "Chad is apparently our one-man welcoming committee." He put his arm around his wife. "This is my wife, Sheila, and these are our girls, Carly and Molly. The young man there is Max, Chad's brother. They belong to my sister and my wife's brother. They're on a trip, so the kids are here for spring break."

"We are double cousins," Chad said, his voice a monotone. "That means we all have the same grandparents."

"I know what double cousins are," Earl said. "I have double cousins too. Haven't seen them in years, but we was pretty tight as kids."

Slim lifted Chad off his shoulders and set him on the floor. "Boy, you're almost too big for that. You'll break my shoulders one of these days." He roughed up Chad's hair. "You should have seen my face when I spotted Earl today. I thought I was dreamin'. I almost pinched myself!"

Earl grinned. "Sure enough was a surprise. How many years has it been?"

Slim rubbed his neck. "Well, we were working on flat roofs in Wyoming that year. It was before the job at the café and after the ranch work . . . I guess it must have been about five years ago."

Earl nodded. "I've missed you, friend. Traveling isn't as much fun without a pardner to watch your back."

Slim's face grew serious. "I'm done traveling, Earl. I've got my friends here and my parents and sister in Colorado. Jumping off the train here in North Platte and going to Pastor Jeff's church around the corner was the best thing I ever did." He shook his head. "But, sometimes I do miss the excitement and friends you make along the way. Like you, Big E." He clapped his friend on the shoulder. "What's the chance of you showing up at the center when I happen to be there?"

"Slim to Nunn," Max said. He doubled over laughing. "I crack myself up!"

"What's so funny?" Chad looked around as everyone else laughed.

Slim grinned. "Earl's last name is Nunn and mine is Slim. Slim to Nunn."

Chad giggled. "Slim to Nunn. Slim to Nunn, it's a pun."

Max smacked his forehead. "What have I done, Slim to Nunn, he'll take it and run . . . "

When the laughter had settled, Aunt Sheila got up and headed for the kitchen. "Well, let me go get ice cream and chocolate syrup and we'll visit some more."

Slim winked at Chad. "You scream, I scream, we all scream for ice cream!"

The room was quiet except for the click of spoons on ice cream bowls. Carly divided her last bite in two with her spoon.

This ice cream is so yummy. Nothing beats plain vanilla with chocolate syrup.

Her mother's voice interrupted her thoughts.

"Do you have enough blankets for both of you, Slim?"

Slim looked up from his bowl. "Yes, ma'am. We do."

Earl put his bowl on the coffee table. "Thanks for letting me crash on Slim's couch, Pastor Jeff. Sure beats the homeless shelter. When my pickup broke down, and I realized it was the water pump, I knew I'd have to stop and earn some money. I could've slept in the pickup, but the nights here are still pretty cold in March, and I didn't want to get in trouble with the law."

"I called my boss, and he said to bring Earl with me Monday," Slim said. "We're roofing next week." He punched Earl in the arm. "Earl here's the one who taught me how to do a tar roof."

Earl winked at Chad. "Taught him everything I knew, back when he was nothing but a greenhorn. Hopefully I'll have my pickup running before too long. I sure do like my own wheels."

Carly looked across the room to Max. He raised his eyebrow, and she knew exactly what he was thinking. Carly squelched a laugh. Daddy had said Earl was shy, but he sure didn't seem to be having trouble talking tonight.

Carly got up to collect the bowls.

"Thank you, Carly," her mom said. "You kids better start working your way through the bathroom. Tomorrow's church. You all need a bath or shower, and I want them done tonight. Sunday mornings are hectic enough—"

"I'll go first," Molly said. "I'm tired."

"I want to wait until after Mom and Dad call." Max looked at the clock. "They said they would call when they get in, and their plane is supposed to land around ten p.m. eastern time."

"Ten-oh-two," Chad said.

"Well, that's nine-oh-two here," Max said. "So, we have at least an hour before we hear from them. Maybe I can get my shower now."

"You can use our bathroom, Max." Carly's dad waved him toward the door. "Bring your towel down from upstairs. If you use both bathrooms, it will go quicker. Just try to stagger them —if you both run water at the same time, someone isn't going to get hot water."

Slim stood and stretched. "Thanks for the ice cream, but we'd better get home. You folks have enough to do. We'll see you in the morning."

Carly watched her dad shake hands with both men. *I sure hope Earl stays. Slim will be sad if he takes off again.* A horrible thought flew through her mind, and she felt like she had been punched in the gut. *What if Slim catches the itch to travel from Earl? He said he's done with that life. But she could tell by how Slim acted they were really good friends. What if Earl talked him into leaving?* Carly shook her head to make the thought go away. *No, that not true. It's not helpful, either. Don't borrow trouble, Carly. Slim wouldn't leave us.* But her unsettled stomach didn't seem convinced.

CHAPTER 5
Pinky's Crew

WHEN CARLY WALKED INTO PINKY'S apartment Monday morning, the pink wasn't quite as overwhelming. The cousins had all decided to wear navy T-shirts and jeans so at least *they* wouldn't be pink.

Kate led the way through the kitchen into the living room. "Thanks for giving me a heads-up about the blue shirts. I like it!" She put one hand on her hip and posed like a model. "Don't you think we look like a professional packing crew, all dressed alike?"

Max laughed. "We need our names on our shirts."

"Embroidered in pink," Molly said.

Aunt Susie laughed. "Okay, Pinky's Crew, where should we start?"

Kate giggled. "Daddy suggested the girls could pack the clothes. Once her closet is empty, we can put packed boxes there." Kate waved her hand toward the kitchen. "We also could start in the kitchen today."

"Then we would have the less interesting stuff done first," Max said.

"What do you mean?" Kate asked.

48

Max shrugged. "I think looking through old papers will be more fun than packing pots, pans, and pink Tupperware, don't you?"

Molly giggled. "I'll help in the kitchen. The pink doesn't bother me."

"I'll work with Molly," Aunt Susie said. "Kitchen stuff can be tricky to pack. We want to get as much into one box as possible. Chad, do you want to help us?"

"Sure thing." Chad tugged at his black hat. "I've got my pink-repelling hat today, so I'll be okay."

Max laughed. "I guess I'll help Carly and Kate." He shuddered. "Old lady clothes."

"Oh, there's tons more in the closet than clothes, Max," Kate assured him. "There are shoe boxes full of letters, important papers, and even old photos. You could start going through them. Plus, someone needs to make boxes and tape the bottoms. Do you know how to do that?" Kate pointed to the flat cardboard boxes leaning against the wall.

"I think I can figure it out." Max looked dubiously at the boxes and the roll of packing tape.

"I'll show you, Max," Aunt Susie said. "You'll catch on quick. It's really quite simple."

"Okay then!" Max rubbed his hands together. "I'll be the box maker for starters, and then I'll do whatever comes up next."

An hour later they had made good progress. The smell of rose-scented powder permeated the bedroom. Carly looked at the boxes of clothes—mostly pink—she and Kate had packed after checking all of the pockets. *How on earth did she not get bored with pink?* She shook her head. *I sure would.*

"Where will you take these clothes?" Carly held the box top shut while Max smoothed one end of the tape onto the box, then pulled the screeching tape dispenser across the top of the box and down the other side. He twisted the dispenser slightly to cut the tape and smoothed it to make sure it was stuck.

"Dad says we'll donate them to the Salvation Army thrift shop," Kate said. "We don't need them, and someone should be able to get some use out of them. I'm saving a couple of things though, some of my favorites. Grandma thought we could make a pillow or something with them."

"Oh, that would be nice!" Carly said. "I'm sure the Salvation Army will be able to use the rest. These clothes are good quality. The store can have an entire pink section!"

"Where can I take these boxes to get them out of the way? The bed's covered, and you can hardly walk around in here for all the boxes." Max leaned against the doorframe.

"I'll take a box and show you," Kate said. "There's a storage room downstairs we don't use much. Dad said to put them there. Then we'll take them over to the Salvation Army when we get time."

Max lifted a box. "These aren't heavy, just bulky; but we'll have to be careful going down the stairs. The boxes will be hard to see over."

February 1943

"You'll like this next stop, soldier." Hy Abram looked out the window to see what the train attendant was talking about. He didn't see anything but more flat prairie.

"Why?" he asked. "What's so special about this place?"

"Why, the whole town turns out to meet you. There's food, coffee, smokes, and pretty girls."

Hy sat up and reached into his pocket for his comb. "If there's going to be pretty girls, I guess I should comb my hair." He looked down at his rumpled uniform pants and T-shirt. "And put on my shirt." He could feel excitement coursing through his veins. The trip from Chicago already seemed interminable, and they still had to go clear to San Francisco. A stop, pretty girls or not, would be a welcome change even if it was just for ten or fifteen minutes.

Ten minutes later when he and his buddies burst through the depot doors, he couldn't believe his eyes, ears, and nose. It was just like being home at a community gathering. Women his mother's age smiled at him from behind piles of sandwiches and plates of cookies. Huge slices of cake begged to be eaten. The smell of coffee—good coffee—almost made him cry. And, yes. He saw pretty girls. One in pink had a smile that could power an entire city block. His eyes lit on the name tag she wore. Pinky. He grinned. Before he got back on that train, he was going to make the acquaintance of Miss Pinky.

By ten-thirty they had packed all the clothes and dishes, only leaving a few paper plates and cups they had found under the counter as well as a pitcher and some napkins. "Just in case we want to eat lunch here one day," Aunt Susie said.

"What should we do now?" Carly sat on the window seat and looked around the living room.

"I think we should go through those shoe boxes we found in the bedroom closet," Kate said. "Let's bring them out here and each take a box. Dad said we need to look in each envelope to see if there's money."

"Money would be good," Chad said with a nod.

Within minutes the group had settled in the living room. The sun shone through the curtains in the double windows that looked out on the street below.

Carly sat cross-legged on the floor and lifted the lid from her box. The now-familiar scent of roses drifted out. The box was crammed with packets of letters, each one tied with plain string. All except one. The last packet in the box had a pink ribbon. Carly picked it up and untied the ribbon. *Why was this one different?* The ribbon dropped into her lap and Carly examined the neat handwriting. Each letter was addressed to Hy Abram at a military address. She leafed through the stack. Every single one was from Pinky Zimmerman of North Platte, Nebraska.

Carly opened the first envelope and looked at the date. *February 25, 1943.* Her eyes scanned the letter.

Dear Hy,

It was a pleasure to meet you at the canteen last week. My sister and I have been volunteering there since Christmas, and you are the first soldier I've written to. Let me tell you a little about myself.

Carly held the letters up. "I've found letters Pinky wrote to your great-grandpa. Did you know they met at the canteen?"

Kate leaned over. "Yes, she told me. Can you believe he kept all of those letters?"

Carly shook her head. "It is a lot of letters." She opened each envelope, pulled out the letter inside—written on such thin paper you could almost see through it—and made sure nothing else was tucked in the letter. Then she refolded it and put it back into its envelope. When she got to the last one, she read it. It made her smile. It was much more personal than the first letter. Pinky was sharing the plans for their wedding. When she finished, Carly straightened the pile and tied the pink ribbon around them again. "You want to keep those, Kate. They are very special."

Kate nodded. "Dad says we'll take them home and next time my grandma and grandpa come from Florida, Grandma can go through things and decide what she wants. If she doesn't want them, I do!"

Carly looked through the other packets. They were all organized according to who had sent them. There were packets from Pinky's mother, her sister Pepper, and other friends. Carly shook her head. "Letters were a big deal back then, I guess."

"There was no such thing as e-mail or cell phones," Aunt Susie said. "Long distance phone calls were expensive, so letters were the cheapest way to communicate." Aunt Susie held up a yellowed newspaper clipping. "This box has a lot of newspaper articles. I've found clippings from World War II, some reporting the bombing of Pearl Harbor, and others from the end of the war. There's even one about President Kennedy's assassination, and another on the Challenger disaster. It's basically a history lesson in a box."

"Let me see that box." Kate reached for it. "I'm going to take it home. I have to pick a major historic event in the past hundred years and do a paper and poster board display about it for my history class."

"Well, I'd say you found your source of information right here!" Aunt Susie handed her the box. "Your Gigi Pinky must have been quite a history buff."

Kate nodded. "She was. She used to meet some of her friends over at Corleigh's Diner across the street every week. They would share new things they learned about history. One of them was the grandpa of my friend at school. His name was Mr. Mayland."

"Wow," Max said. "Do some of them still meet there?"

Kate nodded. "Yes, but there are fewer and fewer. They are either too sick to come or they've died."

"I'm glad your Gigi kept all of this stuff, then," Aunt Susie said.

Max pointed to his box. "You might want to look at this one. It has articles about every presidential election since 1940. There are even notes written on the articles. Apparently your great-grandma did her research before she decided who she would vote for."

Aunt Susie shook her head. "You know, Kate, this could be valuable. I think a museum might be interested in this collection. They're already organized and everything. This would be a treasure trove for anyone writing a book about World War II, presidential elections . . . " Her voice faded and her eyes stared into space.

Carly poked Max in the ribs. Aunt Susie was in the middle of what they called "an author moment." Carly looked over to see if Molly noticed.

Molly sat on the floor, feet straight in front of her, and leaned against the couch. One hand held her place in the pink photo box on her lap. She stared at a picture in her other hand. "Kate, this girl looks like you!" She handed the picture to Kate.

Kate looked at the photo and smiled. "That's my mom. Of course the lady behind her is Pinky; her clothes give her away. The other one is Pepper, and that's Shelly beside my mom. That must have been one of the trips they took." She laughed. "Look, Pinky has her face all screwed up. I bet that's why this picture isn't in a photo album on the shelf over there." She pointed to the bookshelf, overflowing with albums.

Molly put the lid back on the box. "I'm done with these, and all I found were pictures." She jumped up and pulled several photo albums off the shelf. "I'll go through these. I love pictures. And you said we had to look through everything."

Carly giggled. "Sure, Molly. Just doing your job, aren't you?"

Molly made a face at Carly. "That's my story, and I'm sticking to it!"

Chad was the first one to find money. He shouted when he pulled a twenty-dollar bill out of his box of old concert programs. "Money!" He waved the twenty over his head. Everyone cheered.

Aunt Susie grabbed an empty envelope from the pile of office supplies they had started. "Put it in this. We'll keep all the money here as we find it."

By noon the money envelope held two hundred dollars, and the children were more than ready to stop for the day.

"This is hard work," Molly said. "I'm glad we aren't staying all afternoon."

"What are you doing this afternoon?" Kate asked.

"We're going to the Children's Museum. Want to come?" Carly put the lid on her box and added it to the pile of boxes that were finished.

"I'll ask my dad. If I don't, I'll have to stay around here until dad gets off work." Kate said. "I'd rather go with you."

"After the Children's Museum, we need to stop by the library. It's right there, and then we'll walk back home," Molly said.

"I want to look for another book about Buffalo Bill," Chad said. "I'm almost done with the book I got at Fort Cody."

At supper the conversation was lively. The museum had been a big hit with all the hands-on displays and activities. "I thought there would be more local history stuff, though," Max said.

"Me too," said Chad. "I liked the pirate part a lot, but I wanted a Buffalo Bill part."

Uncle Jeff handed the creamed potatoes to Chad. "You'll get more about Buffalo Bill out at his ranch. When are you going there?"

"Tomorrow," Carly said. "The weather is supposed to be nice, so we want to visit the ranch and then go to Cody Park for a while."

A loud knock came from the back door followed by a voice. "Hello!" Kate appeared in the doorway between the kitchen and dining room. "I let myself in. I'm sorry to interrupt, but I have big news and I couldn't wait to tell you."

CHAPTER 6

A Blast from the Past

Chicago, Illinois

The blinking light on the answering machine caught the dark-haired lady's attention as she hurried through the hall. Hmmm. She pushed the button and listened. "Hi, Shelly. This is Nate Neilson. I wanted to let you know we will be cleaning out Pinky's apartment in a week or so. I know you said you wanted to help. We would love to see you. Kate is dying to meet you. Okay. Give our love to your mother. Bye."

The woman stood completely still for a moment, until she was startled back into action by a querulous voice. "Shelly. Shelly, who was that?" The woman hurried into the next room.

"Oh, nothing important. Let's get you your medicine now, okay?" The younger woman smiled at the lady in the rocking chair. "You'll feel much better after a rest."

Kate's face glowed with delight. Carly put down the bowl of peas. *I haven't seen that look on her face for months. Well, not since her Gigi Pinky died, for sure, and I'm not sure she's been this excited since her mom died.*

"What is it?" Carly jumped up and hurried around the table to her friend.

"Mom's cousin Shelly is here! She walked into Dad's office this afternoon while we were at the museum. She said she came to help and to see us. She said her mom's more and more confused, but when she heard Gigi Pinky had died, all she wanted was for Shelly to come. Shelly said she hadn't been able to, but when Dad called and said we would be cleaning out the apartment, she thought she should come help." Kate took a deep breath and went on. "She says I look exactly like my mom did when she was my age."

"Oh, Kate. How wonderful." Carly's mom got up and gave her a hug. "Maybe she'll be able to share more about your mom too. What a wonderful thing!"

"Does she have any idea where to find the necklace?" Max asked.

Kate shrugged. "I don't know. But I'll ask!"

Max looked at Carly. She knew what he was thinking. "Um, maybe you don't need our help then, Kate?" Carly asked. She held her breath.

Kate shook her head. "Oh no. I told her I wanted you to help us. There's plenty to do, and Daddy said if you're willing, we'll take all the help we can get!" She bounced up and down, shaking her arms like she was warming up for a race. Carly could feel the chair under her hand vibrate from the floors bouncing. "I'm so wound up I can't stand still."

Carly laughed. "Will she stay at your house?"

Kate shook her head. "Nope. Dad offered to let her stay at the apartment, but she said she already has a hotel for the week, so she'll stay there."

"What does she look like?" Chad asked. "Does she look like one of those ugly skinny models you see on TV?"

Kate tipped her head sideways. "No." She paused. "She really doesn't look like I expected. She had jeans and a sweatshirt on." She rushed on. "She's really, really nice, and she has long dark hair like my mom had, but she . . . well . . . she doesn't dress up much and she doesn't wear any makeup, and—" She threw her hands in the air. "You'll just have to see for yourself tomorrow."

Carly laughed. "I can't wait to meet her. And I'm glad she came."

"I have to go." Kate turned and headed to the kitchen but continued talking. "We are meeting her at Merrick's Restaurant. She said she used to go there with my mom. They would get a burger basket. So that's what she wants to do. Burger baskets are my favorite too!"

With that she disappeared through the door, calling, "See you in the morning!" The back door slammed.

No one said anything for a minute. It felt like the air had been sucked right out of the room. "Well, I'd say that's one excited girl," Carly's dad said.

"Imagine, having someone who knew your mom when she was little come and visit," Max said. He laughed. "I bet Kate will ask more questions than Chad."

"Hey! What do you mean by that?" Chad glared at his brother. "There you go again saying I ask too many questions. Aunt Sheila said asking questions is a good thing."

The room erupted in laughter.

"Oh, Chad. You ask questions even when you're mad." Carly's mom laughed. "But you are right. I did say that. We like you the way you are, Chad, questions and all."

Max punched his brother in the arm. "Yeah, pest. I wouldn't know what to do if you stopped. Besides, sometimes questions need to be asked."

Chad nodded. "Yep, they sure do. And I have one I want answered."

Carly looked at her dad and she could tell he was almost ready to crack up. "What's that, Chad?"

"Is there dessert tonight? 'Cause I smelled chocolate earlier."

Max rolled his head back onto his chair and groaned. "Oh, Chad. Wait until I tell mom this one."

The next morning at nine o'clock sharp, the cousins hurried up the stairs to the apartment. Max pulled off his jacket as he stepped through the door. Standing in the doorway between the kitchen and living room was a woman he assumed must be Shelly. Kate stood beside her, beaming. *Doesn't look like she's any less excited than last night.*

Max studied the woman. Well, one thing was for sure. She didn't look anything like he thought she would. Oh, she had long dark hair. Her coloring was similar to Kate and to the pictures they had seen yesterday, but she looked . . . hard. Deep lines made paths in her face, and her skin looked tough.

Watching as Kate introduced Carly to Shelly, Max saw that Shelly was kind of clumsy, not at all like you would think of a model. *Of course! She isn't a model. She's a buyer. And, I bet she isn't dressed like she would be if she were going to work. Aunt Susie dresses professional when she has a book signing, but she wore jeans and a sweatshirt today.* He shook his head to redirect his thoughts and stepped forward. He took the lady's hand and smiled. "Kate's sure excited to have you here."

"I'm pleased too," she said, her voice low and scratchy. "I've wanted to make this happen for a lot of years." She put her arm around Kate. "I don't know how Kathy and I lost touch so much that I've never met her husband or her beautiful child."

Max flinched and shot a look at Carly. She was gushing. He hated when people gushed. Carly looked at him, and then looked away. She knew what he was thinking, he could tell.

Aunt Susie hurried into the room. "Did I miss anything while I parked the car?"

Max laughed. "Not really. We were just being introduced."

Aunt Susie held out her hand. "We are so glad you could come. It will be such fun for Kate to learn more about her mom. Childhood friends know all the secrets, don't they?"

Shelly nodded. "They sure do. Well, I guess we should get to work, huh? This place is . . . " Her voice trailed off.

"Pink?" Chad asked. He crept around the living room, looking behind the curtains and the couch.

"Chad, what are you doing?" Max glared at his brother.

"I'm practicing to be a scout like Buffalo Bill. He became such a good scout because he memorized how the prairie looked as he rode. He was observant. I want to be a scout someday, so I need to be more observant."

Molly giggled. "I'll help you practice. Later this afternoon I'll ask you where stuff is in this apartment, and we'll see how observant you were."

The morning flew by. They managed to go through all the boxes from the closet and finished the bedroom. All that was left were the knickknacks on top of the dresser. Carly admired the jewelry box resting in the exact center of the dresser. She ran her fingers over the waxed wood. *I've never seen one this beautiful before.* She lifted the lid and the scent of cedar drifted out. A mass of necklaces and pins filled the box. The necklaces were mostly pink. No surprise there, but Carly spotted a few multicolor pieces. *It all looks like costume jewelry.*

Something caught her eye. Poking out from under the corner of the box she saw a piece of paper. She pulled it out. It was an envelope. "Hey, here's a letter from Shelly to Gigi Pinky." She handed the letter to Kate.

Kate glanced at the addresses and tucked it in her jeans pocket. "I'll give it to Shelly later. I bet she'll want it." She rubbed her hand along the top of the dresser. "I guess we should pack these things into a box. My grandma will have to decide what to do with them." Kate grabbed a small box and taped the bottom shut. "Then we'll be done in here."

Carly nodded. "I wonder what made Pinky wear pink all the time. A lot of people like a color, but this seems so—well, over the top."

Kate nodded. "I don't know. I asked her once and she just tossed her head, threw her pink scarf over her shoulder and announced, 'I was born to be Pinky.'"

Carly giggled. "I'm beginning to feel really bad I didn't spend more time with your great-grandma, Kate."

"Carly, come here." Max's voice filled the apartment.

"I guess I better see what he wants." Carly hurried out of the bedroom. In the hallway she almost ran into Shelly standing in front of the plastic case, staring at the Russian coin and the letter. Shelly jumped.

"This really is special, isn't it?" the woman said.

Carly nodded. "Yep, it's a treasure, for sure!"

"Oh, my!" Shelly shook her head. "It should be in a museum. I bet a museum would pay big bucks for that."

Carly shrugged. "I guess. Excuse me. Max called me." She hurried into the living room where Max waved some money over his head. "Look what I found. A hundred-dollar bill!"

Carly's eyes popped wide open! "Whoa! Where'd you find that?"

"In the junk drawer in the kitchen," Max said. Kate and Shelly hurried into the room, drawn by the excited voices. Max handed it to Kate. "Here you go. One hundred dollars."

Kate held it flat in both of her hands and stared at it. "Wow! I've never held this much money before." Carly grabbed the envelope off the coffee table and held it out. Kate slipped the bill in and laid it back on the table. "That's four hundred and thirty dollars so far. That's a lot of money," Kate said.

"Sure is," Aunt Susie said. She looked at her watch. "It's about lunch time."

Heavy footsteps came up the stairs, and Carly turned toward the kitchen. Around the corner and into the apartment walked Slim and Earl, each with a large pizza box.

"Pizza, pizza, pizza, pizza!" crowed Chad. "I love pizza."

Earl and Slim froze in place and looked around. Slim shook his head. "That's a lot of pink!" He came into the living room and put the pizza on the coffee table. Earl placed his beside Slim's. Slim opened both boxes and put napkins beside them. "Eat up. Your Aunt Susie texted a plea for help, and here we are."

Carly hugged Slim. "Thanks, guys. This is great." She turned to thank Earl, but he was staring at Shelly. Carly couldn't quite figure out the look on his face, maybe a bit uncertain. Carly looked at Shelly. Her eyes were firmly planted on the floor and she was pale as a ghost.

"We have four hundred and thirty dollars in that envelope," Chad pointed to the envelope on the coffee table.

Max rolled his eyes. "It doesn't belong to us, Chad. It belongs to Dr. Nate." Max saw Earl's eyes swing over to the envelope.

Kate shook her head. "Actually, it belongs to my grandma in Florida, but she told Dad that any cash we find can help renovate the apartment. We'll need lots of paint, and it won't be pink." She picked up the envelope and peeked inside, then put it back on the table beside the pizza boxes. "Wish it was mine. I'd get a new pair of ice skates."

The living room was crowded with the four adults and five children. The smell of fresh pizza filled the room. Max took a bite of pepperoni pizza and closed his eyes. *This is so good!*

Within minutes, the pizza was gone. Slim wiped his hands on a napkin, gulped down the rest of his water, and stretched. "We better get going. We're supposed to meet my boss at a work site for the afternoon." He and Earl headed for the door. The rest of the group jumped up and hurried out to the kitchen to throw out their napkins. In the tiny apartment, it caused a traffic jam, and by the time everyone got done, the whole group was laughing. After a round of cheerful good-byes, Slim and Earl hurried down the stairs and out the back door.

"That was yummy," Carly said. "Thanks for the pizza, Aunt Susie."

Shelly threw the pizza boxes in the big black trash bag they had been using for trash. "Yeah, thanks." She wiped her hands on her jeans.

"You're welcome," Aunt Susie said. "I thought it might speed things up this afternoon. If we're going to get to Buffalo Bill's house, we had better hit the road."

"How's it coming up here?" Dr. Nate appeared in the doorway between the kitchen and the living room. "I heard a lot of action up here through the floor. Did you get a bunch done?"

Kate hugged her dad. "We sure did. We're done in the bedroom, except for the things on top of the dresser. We just had pizza with Slim and Earl, his friend. Oh," she turned to the coffee table, "we found a bunch of money too. We have four hundred and thirty . . . " Her voice faded, and she hurried over to the table.

Max stared at the coffee table. The spot where Kate had put the envelope was empty. The money was gone.

CHAPTER 7

A Cloud of Suspicion

KATE BEGAN SHUFFLING THROUGH THE papers on the coffee table. Carly, unable to believe her eyes, hurried over and picked up another pile. One by one she laid the papers on the table. No envelope.

"It was here when we were eating." Kate's hands shook. "Right there." She pointed to the spot. "It was right beside the pizza boxes."

"I'll look in the trash." Aunt Susie hurried to the bag. "I bet it got picked up with the pizza boxes."

Carly felt her shoulders relax. *Of course, that's where it is.* The group gathered around Aunt Susie as she looked. No one made a sound while Aunt Susie completely emptied the bag, removing everything and placing it in another bag. No money.

Dr. Nate shrugged and put his hands in the pockets of his lab coat. "I wouldn't get too excited about it yet. I'm sure it's around here somewhere. It probably got shoved under something, or picked up with another pile."

Shelly shook her head. "It was right there on the table." Carly flinched at the harsh, angry tone of the woman's voice. "I bet one of those guys took it."

Carly gasped and she felt the blood drain out of her face. "Slim wouldn't steal anything!" The words burst out of her. She looked at Max. His face was beet red. He was furious.

"That's right," Max said. "Slim would not steal that money. And I don't think Earl would either."

Chad marched over to Shelly and stopped in front of her. "That's not very nice. Blaming them when they aren't even here to defend themselves. I don't like you."

"Chad," Aunt Susie said, her voice quiet but firm. "You don't talk to Shelly like that."

"Well, I didn't take it," Shelly said. "Did any of you?"

Carly looked around. Everyone shook their head no.

"Now, now." Dr. Nate held up his hand. "We won't be laying blame here. Don't get too excited about this. The money will show up. We'll check with Slim and Earl this evening. It's possible they accidently picked it up with their stuff."

Shelly shook her head and mumbled under her breath. Kate burst into tears and ran out of the apartment and down the stairs.

Max rode beside Aunt Susie. Her hands clenched the wheel so tight her knuckles turned white. Her face was pale, and Max had never seen her lips that tight. She looked like she was trying really hard not to say something. "Aunt Susie, can we go back to Carly's house?" he said. "I don't want to go to the

Buffalo Bill house this afternoon. I'm too mad and upset. I won't enjoy it at all."

She looked straight ahead. "That's a good idea." Max heard her phone buzz like she had a message. She didn't look down. She just drove.

"Well, I know Slim didn't take it," Chad said. Max glanced into the back. Chad slouched down in the seat, his arms crossed, chin stuck out. Carly and Molly said nothing. Tears trickled down Molly's face.

Aunt Susie looked in the rearview mirror. "I agree, Chad. But, someone took that money, or it's mislaid. Either way, we need to find it."

Max couldn't think of anything to say, so he didn't. *Like Dad says, we can only know for sure what we do or what we see someone else do. I didn't take it, and I didn't see anyone else take it, so I can't be one-hundred percent sure who did or didn't.* His mind raced on. *I totally don't think anyone in my family did it. Slim neither.* He leaned his head against the window. *And why would Kate take it? That just leaves Shelly and Earl.* He chewed on his lip. *I sure hope Earl didn't take it.*

And what about Shelly? His heart sank. He just didn't have a good feeling about her, but he didn't know why. Grandpa Johnson would say, "I can't quite put my finger on it."

Despite the situation, a smile snuck its way onto his face. *I wish Grandpa was here. He would have something helpful to say.* Max's eyes narrowed again as he thought about Shelly. *Wasn't it strange she showed up right when they were cleaning out the house?* He argued with himself. *I do jump to conclusions about people. I don't want to do what I did when I first met Slim, before we knew we were distant cousins! And Kate's dad did call and let Shelly know they were cleaning out the apartment.*

The car pulled up to the house, and Aunt Susie put it in park. She picked up her phone and looked at the message. "It's from Slim," she said. "I texted him before we left the apartment. He said they looked through their stuff, and they don't have it. He says he trusts Earl completely."

"That just leaves Shelly," Max said.

Aunt Susie unbuckled her seatbelt. "We don't know for sure, Max. But we need to pray that money shows up."

Aunt Susie had texted Carly's dad too, and by the time they got in the house, Carly's parents were waiting. Max dropped onto the couch. He saw Carly open her mouth to tell her parents about it, but everyone started to talk at once.

Uncle Jeff held up his hand. "I spoke to Dr. Nate already. He's not worried about it. He believes the money will show up. But he does want to talk to Slim and Earl. I promised I'll go with him tonight. I don't think Slim took it, nor do I believe anyone in this room did."

"I sure didn't!" Chad's eyes were huge.

"Me neither." Molly leaned against her mom's arm. "It was right there in front of us. How could anyone take it without being seen, anyway?"

Max shook his head. "I have no idea. But I know I didn't take it."

"Me either," Carly said.

Aunt Susie rubbed her forehead. "Well, I sure didn't. I really can't imagine anyone in that room taking it, that's the thing. Why would they?"

Carly's dad nodded. "That's a good question. Nate doesn't want to call the police. He's a peace-loving guy, and he'd rather work it out among us. I hope we can."

"I think you kids should go upstairs and watch a movie or read a book. You need a little down time." Aunt Sheila pushed Molly's hair back.

Max felt Carly shudder beside him on the couch. "I guess," she said. "I just want this over with. Having a cloud of suspicion hanging over our heads is scary."

Carly's dad nodded. "Yes, yes, it is."

Carly sat on the couch upstairs and pretended to watch *Akeelah and the Bee*. Molly chose it because Dorie was at the national spelling bee. Carly had seen it several times and loved it, but she couldn't concentrate. *How could this happen?* Max poked her in the side and tipped his head sideways. Carly eased off the couch. Molly and Chad didn't even notice them leave.

Carly slid down the wall and sat on the playroom floor by the dollhouse. She stared at Max, and he stared back. Neither of them said a word for what seemed to Carly like forever.

"I don't trust that Shelly," Max said. He almost spit the words.

Max's fierceness startled Carly. His face was red as a beet again.

"I've tried to like her and not to jump to conclusions but something's not right." Max ran his hand through his hair.

Carly nodded. "I know what you mean. She doesn't quite fit, does she? And she was so quick to blame Slim and Earl." Carly snapped her fingers. "Another thing. She kept staring at that coin and the letter in the hall. She said it would be worth a lot of money."

Max's mouth fell open. "She said that?"

Carly nodded. "And something else. I think she knows Earl. She looked like she had seen a ghost when he came in. And when he was introduced to her, he looked confused, kind of. Like he thought she was someone else."

Max shook his head. "What do you think that means?"

"I have no idea. I just feel like she isn't telling us the truth about something, but I don't know what."

Max leaned his head on his hand. "But, to be fair, we don't know much about Earl either. I want to believe he didn't do it 'cause he's Slim's friend, but Slim hasn't seen him for five years. And Earl does need money."

Carly nodded. "That money would go a long way toward fixing his pickup. But if he used it for that, everyone would *know* he stole the money. That doesn't make sense."

Max's face lit up. "You're right. I really hate the thought that Slim's friend could be a thief!"

"And Kate doesn't want to believe her mom's best childhood friend would take it," Carly said. "Kate is so upset. I feel terrible." She put her head down on her knees and took some deep breaths.

"Well, if I was Earl, I sure wouldn't stick around," Max said.

Carly's head snapped up. "I know. I'm worried if Earl gets blamed he'll take off. And how will Slim feel? They are such good friends, kind of like brothers. What if Slim decides to go with Earl?" Carly chewed her fingernail. A lump that felt the size of Nebraska lodged in her throat. "What are we going to do? We can't let that happen!"

"We could make cookies."

Carly looked up and saw Molly leaning against the doorway. "I want to make no-bake chocolate cookies," Molly said. "Want to help? I thought we could give some to Kate and her dad, and even Shelly. And some to Slim and Earl." Molly shifted from one foot to another. "So they all know we aren't mad at them."

Carly nodded. "Sure, I'll help, Molly. I've got to keep busy or I'll go crazy."

Chad appeared behind Molly. "Can I help? What are we doing?"

Max laughed. "You don't even know what's happening and you want to help." He shook his head. "Crazy boy."

Chad stuck his tongue out. "I'm a helpful boy. Besides, sitting around is no fun."

Carly jumped up. "Hey, maybe Mom hasn't started supper yet. If she hasn't, you and I could fix macaroni and cheese, Max; and Molly and Chad could make cookies. Doesn't mac and cheese sound good?"

"Oh yeah," Max said. "Let's ask. And while we cook, we can see if we can think of ways to solve the mystery of this missing money."

CHAPTER 8

Guilt and Innocence

CARLY TOOK A BITE OF macaroni and cheese made with Velveeta and milk and let it sit in her mouth for a moment. *I love macaroni and cheese. Nothing bad can happen when you are eating mac and cheese, can it?* She giggled.

"This macaroni and cheese is wonderful," Carly's mom said. "Thanks for fixing supper. Twice this week. You're going to spoil me."

"I can't wait to have one of those cookies I saw in the kitchen," Carly's dad said, gazing longingly into the kitchen. "The smell of chocolate nearly drove me crazy this afternoon." He made his crazy man face, and all the kids cracked up.

"It was Molly's idea," Carly said. "She wanted to give some cookies to the Neilsons, Shelly, Slim, and Earl." Carly felt the tension start to creep up through her shoulders again.

"That's very thoughtful, Molly." Carly's mom folded her napkin and laid it beside her plate. "I know you kids are worried about this mess with the money. But, I think the truth will come out."

"After Slim gets home from class, he and Earl are coming over," Carly's dad said. "Nate's coming too. He said he would bring Kate with him. Maybe you kids can hang out upstairs while we talk."

"Can we have hot chocolate with our cookies?" Carly asked.

"Sure," her mom said. "Unless you think that's too much chocolate."

Carly shook her head. "That's not possible."

At seven-thirty, the cousins and Kate gathered on the big couch upstairs. The fire flickered and crackled, and Carly snuggled down under her favorite fleecy snowflake blanket. This would be a perfect evening if it weren't for the conversation she knew they were having downstairs. She handed the plate of cookies to Kate, picked up her mug, and inhaled the scent of hot chocolate.

Kate took a cookie and passed the plate on to Molly. "I'm sure glad Dad let me come over here. I've been dying to talk to you guys all afternoon."

"Why?" Max leaned forward and snagged a cookie off the plate, sat back, and took a bite.

Kate looked at the ceiling. "Where should I start? Okay. After you left, Dad said he thought we should stop cleaning out the apartment for now. He said it's too much drama. He asked us to look for the envelope because he doesn't believe anyone took it. He thinks we misplaced it."

"Misplaced it? That's crazy!" Max stared at Kate. "We all saw it on the table."

"I know, right?" Kate shook her head. "That's what I told him. After he went downstairs for his next appointment, Shelly went off. She ranted about how she didn't like Earl. She's sure he took the money." Kate's chin quivered. She sat up straighter and took a deep breath. "She used words my mom never let me say. She went on and on. It kind of scared me." Kate put her face in her hands and cried.

Carly handed her a tissue from the box on the end table and raised her eyebrows at Molly. Kate hardly ever cried.

"Did you tell your dad?" Carly asked. "He wouldn't want you to be hollered at."

Kate wiped off the tears with angry jerks. "Sorry, guys. I feel like a cry-baby." Her eyes narrowed. "No, I didn't tell my dad. He was so excited about Shelly coming. He told me he's worried that I need a woman around, and he hopes Shelly will be able to make me feel connected to my mom." She threw up her hands. "I want to like Shelly. I really do, but she's so rude sometimes. I can't imagine that she and my mom were friends." Her voice trailed off. "But she is family, you know?"

Carly nodded. "Yes, and she may feel like we blame her too. Maybe that's why she's so pushy."

Kate shrugged. "I don't know. But we spent all afternoon searching the apartment for the money, and it's gone. Someone took it. It sure didn't walk away by itself."

"So what are we going to do about it?" Molly asked.

Max pointed to Chad, engrossed in the Buffalo Bill book he had checked out of the library with Molly's card. "I think we all need to take a lesson from Buffalo Bill," Max said.

"Huh?" Chad looked up from his book. "What did you say?"

"Well, you said Buffalo Bill was a great scout. That he learned by observation. We have to be scouts. We need to observe, observe, observe." He sat up straighter. "We should each try and remember what we saw earlier today at lunch. Where you were when we finished lunch? Because that money was there during lunch, but right after, it was gone."

Chad put his book down. "Well, I told Slim and Earl about it during lunch." He frowned. "Maybe I shouldn't have said anything about it," Chad said, his eyes huge.

"I wouldn't worry about that," Carly said.

"After Chad said that, I picked up the envelope and looked at it," Kate said.

"And I saw you put it back down, right by the pizza box." Carly shut her eyes and imagined herself back in the room. "Then Slim said they had to leave."

The room fell silent. Carly ran the scene through her head, over and over. "It got kind of chaotic then because Aunt Susie said we should go. We all got up and tried to put our stuff away at once."

Max shook his head. "No, I don't think Aunt Susie said anything about leaving until everyone was already up. When your dad came in, wasn't it, Kate?"

Carly nodded. "Yeah, you're right, Max."

"Slim and Earl went into the kitchen first," Chad said. "They didn't go back into the living room because they stood in the kitchen and talked to Aunt Susie. When I went out there, I stayed to listen. I was scouting."

Max laughed. "You just wanted to hang around Slim."

Chad shrugged. "But I was scouting too. Then Slim and Earl left."

"So if Earl's the thief, he had to take it before they left the room," Carly said.

"I waited kind of till the end to throw my stuff away," Kate said. "Everyone was trying to go at once, so I waited. You were with me, Molly."

Molly nodded. "Yep, you, me, and Shelly were the last ones in the living room. Then we both grabbed our plates and went into the kitchen. That's when Carly and Max went back into the living room."

"When we went back in, Shelly was just inside the living room. She had her plate in her hand. She was the last one in the living room," Carly said. She closed her eyes and imagined the room. "The pizza boxes were still on the table though. That's when Shelly turned around and grabbed the boxes." Carly pulled her hair. "Argh. I just wish I could remember if the envelope was there then."

The room grew silent.

The quiet was shattered by a commotion downstairs. "I did not take that money. I've told you over and over, I am not a thief. I don't lie. Just because I'm a transient, that doesn't make me a thief." It was Earl.

Other voices murmured a response, then silence followed by heavy footsteps stomping through the downstairs. Max slipped over to the back window and lifted it. The others hunched down around him on the stairs. The back door slammed open, and Earl tore down the back steps, closely followed by Slim. Slim grabbed his friend's arm.

"Earl, if you get mad and run, you'll look guilty as sin. I believe you, but you have to wait it out." Slim stared his friend down.

Earl smashed his baseball cap on his head. "Yeah, and if I stay around here I'll end up in jail for a crime I didn't do. I'm out of here."

"Your pickup isn't fixed. You've got to wait it out, man." Slim's voice was controlled but firm. "I'm telling you. They're good people. They don't want to blame you just because you are transient. I trust them like I trust you. Don't go, please."

Earl stared at Slim. "I wish I could believe you're right, Slim. I know you trust me. But you aren't one of us anymore, are ya?" He kicked at the grass in the yard. "And you aren't really one of them either."

Slim looked like he had been slapped. Molly grabbed Carly's arm and squeezed so hard it hurt.

"That's where you are wrong, Earl," Slim said. "*I am* one of them. They are my family. I would trust them with my life, like I trust you. You've got to believe me. I have your back, man."

Earl looked at his feet and finally shrugged. "I don't know. I just don't know." He turned and lumbered down the pathway to the apartment. Slim stuck to him like glue, still talking.

Max slid the window shut, and the kids went back to the couch.

"What a mess," Max said.

Carly shuddered. "I sure hope Earl doesn't leave."

"Me too," Max said. "But that's Slim's battle. What are we going to do tomorrow? I take it we aren't working at the apartment."

"Nope," Kate said. "I told my dad I wanted to spend the day with you guys."

Carly nodded. "I don't blame you. Maybe Shelly will calm down. I think we're going to the museum and Buffalo Bill's house. I'm sure Aunt Susie won't mind if you come."

Kate looked relieved. "I would like that."

"Why don't you invite Shelly to come?" Molly suggested, her voice uncertain.

"Why on earth would she invite her?" Max asked.

"I think it might be a good idea," Carly said. "If she is there, we can be scouts and keep our eyes open."

Max's face lit up. "Oh, I get it. Well, we better ask Aunt Susie. I don't think she likes Shelly much since she practically accused Slim of stealing the money."

"Yeah, she was pretty mad." Carly put her head in her hands. "I'm tired. Drama, drama, drama! It just wears me out!"

"Kate, your dad's ready to go." The kids jumped when they heard Carly's mom call up the stairs.

"Okay! I'll be right down!" Kate called. She leaned over and gave Carly a hug. "I don't think it was Earl," she said, her voice a fierce whisper. "Family or not, I think it might be Shelly. Call your Aunt Susie and let me know in the morning."

The next morning, Carly climbed into the back of Aunt Susie's SUV and slid across the seat. She shivered in the cool morning air and crossed her arms to hold more heat in. Mom said it was supposed to warm up by noon. She hoped so. She looked at the little purple flowers blooming in the flower bed by the street. Spring was finally here!

Kate slid in beside Carly.

"I'm sure glad you could come, Kate. Is Shelly coming?"

Kate nodded. "I called her this morning. She told me to text her when we leave, and she'll meet us." She shrugged. "I told her we could come pick her up or she could come here, but she said she wanted to go to the store first."

Carly leaned over and whispered in her friend's ear. "Maybe she'll be nicer today."

Kate nodded. "If she's not, at least I won't be by myself."

Moments later the cousins and Kate were belted in and on their way. This time, though, Carly's mom sat in the front passenger seat.

"Thanks for coming along, Sheila," Aunt Susie said, and smiled at Carly's mom.

"My pleasure." Carly's mom touched Aunt Susie's arm lightly. "It's always a good day when I get to spend it with you and my favorite kids."

Carly looked out the window and watched as the SUV turned to go over the viaduct. "I'm glad we're visiting the Buffalo Bill house first," she said. "Max and Chad will love it, especially the barn. Sometimes there is even an actor who is dressed like Buffalo Bill."

"Do you think he'll be there today?" Chad bounced in his seat.

"I doubt it," said Carly's mom. "That's more in the summer."

"Oh." Chad slumped in his seat.

"What's so great about the barn?" Max asked.

"It's the original one," Carly said. "I don't remember the details, but for one thing, it's painted white inside, and that makes it bright and clean. And there's a carving and posters and saddles and other memorabilia. They kept some of their food stored out there in the olden days. It's not like any barn I've ever seen anywhere else."

"It looks massive in the pictures," Max said.

"It is." Molly turned sideways in the middle seat where she sat with Max and Chad. "I love the house. It's so elegant. All of those little old-fashioned designs on the outside are so pretty."

"Elegant, smelligant," Chad said. "I'll stick with the barn."

"So, Chad, tell us more about Buffalo Bill," Aunt Susie said as she looked at him in the rearview mirror.

"Well," Chad said, "he was a scout for different people taking supplies out West. He rode for the Pony Express. He was really good at avoiding Indians and not getting killed. He made friends with a lot of Native Americans. He always wanted to be honest with them." Chad stopped for a breath and then continued. "He scouted for the Army at Fort McPherson, over by Maxwell. His family even lived there. And that's how he discovered that he liked it here. He decided to build a place where he could rest. Then he started his Wild West."

"You mean his Wild West Show?" Max asked.

Chad shook his head. "The word *show* wasn't in the title when he did it. He wanted people to see what the West was like. He was smart, 'cause he knew things were changing. He was afraid people wouldn't know how it really was. He wanted them to be able to see it, hear it, and even smell it."

"Wow, I never knew any of that, and I live here," Molly said. "You're like a Wikipedia article, Chad. You must have memorized those books you are reading."

Chad beamed. "It's interesting. Did you know that when he built the house here, he wanted trees, but he couldn't get any to grow because there's only three feet of dirt over the rock layer underground?"

"Only three feet? Wow!" Max said. "But isn't there a massive lake under Nebraska?"

Carly nodded. "Yep, the Ogallala Aquifer."

"We're studying that in school right now," Kate said.

"So are we," Carly said. "Isn't that weird?" Carly and Molly attended a private school, but Kate went to Washington Elementary School, two blocks from their homes.

Kate nodded. "I had to do a map of the area that covers the aquifer. It's underneath parts of seven states, but Nebraska has the most. If you look at the map, there's just a tiny section back east that doesn't have it." Her voice sobered. "Thirty percent of the irrigation water in the country comes from the aquifer, and the levels are dropping. If we use it all up, it will take six thousand years for it to build back up from rainwater!"

"Whoa!" Chad's eyes were as big as saucers. "I guess I better hurry when I'm in the shower!"

Aunt Susie nodded. "Yep, water conservation is important. Well, we've arrived."

Carly looked out the window as Aunt Susie stopped in front of the beautiful green-trimmed home Buffalo Bill had built. The balconies and towers took her breath away every time she looked at it. "Chad, can you finish telling us about the trees later?" Carly asked.

"Not much more to tell." Chad unhooked his seat belt and pushed the door open. "They just had to find trees that didn't need deep soil, ones that could send their roots out kinda sideways. Once they found them, everyone else in the area planted the same kind."

"Then they must have been cottonwood, box elder, and locust trees," Kate said. "Like what we have in our neighborhood."

Chad nodded. "Yep."

Carly stepped out of the vehicle and unzipped her windbreaker. "It's already warming up. What's the temperature supposed to be?"

"I think in the mid-sixties," Aunt Susie said.

A small economy car pulled in beside them. "Here's Shelly." Kate stepped closer to Carly.

Shelly popped out of the car, a huge smile plastered on her face. "Isn't this fabulous?" She threw her arms wide and gazed at the house. "Out of all the places your mom and I saw with our grandmas, this was my favorite." She turned to Aunt Susie and Carly's mom. "Don't you think it's just extravagant? So classy." She held out her hand to Carly's mom. "I don't think we have met. I'm Shelly Samuelson. Thank you so much for including me today."

Carly glanced at Kate. Her mouth hung open. When she saw Carly looking at her, she snapped it shut and turned her back on Shelly.

Kate rolled her eyes at Carly and Max. "She's gushing again," she muttered.

"At least she's not angry," Max whispered.

"I'm ready to go see this place," Kate said. She stomped up the path to the front door.

"That Kate. So much like her mom," Shelly said. She hurried after Kate. "How are you this morning, sweetheart?"

Carly stuck close to Kate's side. No way was she leaving her friend alone. Not with such an unpredictable person around.

CHAPTER 9

Cody Park

IT WAS A COUPLE OF hours before the group returned to their cars. Max watched as Chad, giddy with excitement over all he had seen, bounced from one spot to another, chattering so fast it was almost impossible to understand him. "That barn's a-double-mazing," he said. "I saw so much Buffalo Bill stuff! The posters, the buggies, the stagecoaches, the saddles—" Chad threw his arms out. "I love this place!" Suddenly, Chad jerked to a stop. He gulped a time or two, then announced, "When I grow up I want to work here. I wish I had lived when Buffalo Bill did! I would have hunted and traveled with him."

"Somehow I can see that happening, Chad," Aunt Susie said. She pulled Chad in for a side hug. "But I'm glad God put you here now, instead."

"Chad, get in the car," Max said. He held the door open. "We're waiting for you."

Shelly peered at Kate in the back seat.

"Was everything how you remembered, Shelly?" Max asked.

"Oh, I don't know." She tossed her head. "It was such a long time ago, you know?" She put her hands on her hips and spoke

86

through the car window. "Kate, I thought you would want to go with me!"

Max glanced into the back seat and saw Kate grab Carly's hand.

"Oh, thanks, Shelly," Kate said. "I'm here now. I'll just ride with Carly and Molly."

Max smiled at Shelly. "Are you going with us over to the museum?"

Aunt Susie held out her iPhone. "Their website says they aren't open until May."

"What?" Carly cried from the back seat. "Argh!"

Carly's mom chuckled. "Well, that's life. I have an idea. Let's go to the park. I don't think we'll get nicer weather."

"Oh, goody," Molly said. "I love the peacocks. They're gorgeous when they open up their tails into those beautiful fans. Maybe I can even find a feather that's fallen off. I'm collecting them."

"Awesome," Max said. "The park is my favorite place in North Platte. There's a ton to see and do."

"Well, remember the rides aren't open this time of year, and there won't be cotton candy," Aunt Susie said. "Just a plain old park in early spring."

Max grinned. "That's okay. I feel like a walk. Maybe even a run!"

"And they have a life-sized statue of Buffalo Bill, Chad," Aunt Susie said.

"Wahoo! Let's *go*," Chad said. "Can you take a picture on your phone for me, Aunt Susie? A picture of me with Buffalo Bill?"

Aunt Susie laughed. "I guess I can." She turned to Shelly. "You want to follow us over there?"

Shelly shrugged. "Sure. Might as well."

Ten minutes later, Aunt Susie pulled through Cody Park entrance and drove along the row of flags from different states. She parked along the edge of the road, across from the Ferris wheel and carousel. Carly peered out the window. A tarp covered the carousel, completely hiding the beautiful historic ride. The Ferris wheel, all pink and purple, loomed above them, waiting patiently for summer. Two workmen bustled around the equipment.

"When do they open for the season?" Molly asked.

"I think April," her mother said. "But just for the weekends."

"That's next week," Max said. "But we'll be back home already. No ice cream, nachos, pretzels, or cotton candy this time."

"You should come in September," Carly said. "That's when they have the big event out here. It's a huge festival with booths and rides. They have bands and music almost all day."

"Maybe we can come next fall," Max said. "Aunt Susie, do you have any sports stuff in the back of your SUV?"

"I did last time I checked." Aunt Susie went around to the back and lifted the door. "Here's a Frisbee and a small Cornhuskers football."

"Want to play Frisbee, Carly?" Max asked.

"Sure." Carly peeled off her jacket. "Do you want to play too, Kate?"

Before Shelly even pulled into the parking spot behind them, the kids were engrossed in a game of Frisbee. After a few minutes, Carly looked over and saw the three women leaning against the SUV. Shelly threw her head back and laughed at something Aunt Susie said. So friendly.

Maybe we have been too hard on her. After all, she's the outsider. We should be nicer to her.

"Hey, where are they going?" Kate pointed toward the vehicles. Aunt Susie hadn't moved, but Carly's mom and Shelly were climbing into Shelly's car.

"I don't know." Carly held her hand over her eyes to block the sun. She waved at her mom, and then hollered to Aunt Susie. "Where are they going?"

"For lunch. They're going to your house for food, and then they'll be back." Aunt Susie jogged out to the kids. "Can I play?"

Fifteen minutes later, the kids had tired of Frisbee. Carly, Kate, and Molly sprawled on the grass and stared at clouds while Max and Chad tossed the football back and forth. Carly could smell the moist dirt, and she felt the dampness soaking through her shirt and jeans, but she didn't care. The sun was so warm that she felt a bit drowsy. Aunt Susie leaned up against a locust tree. Carly watched her pull apart a dark brown pod, nine inches long, that had dropped off the tree. Carly looked up at the tree where more pods hung, ready to let loose and fall to the ground. They made her feel creepy, like something out of a dark forest in a scary movie. She shuddered. So much for relaxing. She liked locust trees much better in the summer when they were covered with green leaves.

"Aunt Susie, will you go with me over to the statue to get my picture with Buffalo Bill now?" Chad begged. "I have to get a picture."

"Sure! Anyone else want to go?" Aunt Susie pushed herself up and stared down at the kids. She crossed her arms. "Surely you aren't more tired than me!"

Molly jumped up. "I'll go. I'd like a photo with the famous gentleman too! Besides, I saw some peacocks over that way when we pulled in. Maybe I'll find my feather. I'd rather go with someone 'cause the geese scare me. They chased me once." Molly shuddered. "And they stink."

Carly, Max, and Kate shook their heads. "We'll stay here and guard the SUV," Max said. He plopped down beside Carly. "We'll make sure nothing happens to it. We've got this."

Aunt Susie laughed. "Oh, good. I'm so relieved."

Carly watched as Aunt Susie, Chad, and Molly walked across the park toward the statue at the entrance. Kate sat up. "Shelly's making me feel crazy today. She's being ultra-nice. Was I all wrong?"

Carly sat up and hugged her knees. "I know. She sure is different. Maybe she was just afraid she would get blamed for the missing money."

Max shook his head. "I don't know, I still think something is off. I think the nice Shelly is an act."

Kate nodded. "I agree. The mean Shelly seemed way more natural, believe me." She sighed. "It's been almost fifteen years since my mom last saw Shelly. People can change a lot in fifteen years."

Carly scratched a circle in the ground with a little stick. "That's true."

"Well, thanks for letting me hang out with you today. I wonder what she and your mom are talking about. I'd love to be a fly on the wall, Carly."

"I know," Carly said. "I thought about asking if I could go, just so I could hear. But, I bet they wouldn't talk about the same stuff with me in the car."

"I don't know what they're talking about, but I sure hope they get back with lunch soon," Max said. "I'm hungry."

Shelly's car pulled up behind Aunt Susie's just as Aunt Susie, Chad, and Molly got back. Chad, Aunt Susie's phone in his hand, hurried over to Max. "Look at this picture! I'm going to text it to Mom and Dad."

Max took the phone and laughed. In the picture, Chad looked like he had just been told he'd won a chocolate store. Max gave his brother a high five. "Mom and Dad will love it." He handed the phone to Aunt Susie and jogged over to the car. "Can I help carry something? We've got a picnic table picked out." He pointed to the table under the locust tree.

Shelly looked surprised. "Sure. What a nice kid. Thanks."

Aunt Sheila winked at Max. "He *is* a good kid. Here, Max. You carry the thermos and paper products."

Max grabbed the stuff and hurried toward the table. Aunt Sheila and Shelly followed him. He set them down on the table.

"Anybody hungry?" Aunt Sheila asked. "We've got sandwiches, apples, baby carrots, chips, and cookies. That should keep you from starving."

"Sounds good, Mom." Carly swung one leg over the bench, then the other, and sat down. "I'm still disappointed we couldn't go to the depot museum today, but this is fun."

"There's a book at Gigi Pinky's about the depot," Kate said. "It's all about how the town kept the canteen going all through the war. I don't remember the title, but I know exactly where to find it. I'll ask Daddy if you can borrow it."

"It's called *Once upon a Town*," Aunt Susie said. "We could go downtown too and see where the depot stood. There's a nice plaque on the site."

"What was the big deal about the depot?" Shelly bit into her sandwich.

Max saw Kate's hand stop, halfway to her mouth. She lowered the sandwich and stared at Shelly. "You know, *the* depot. The one where your Grandma Pepper and my Gigi Pinky volunteered during the war? The one where they both met their husbands," Kate almost shouted.

Shelly froze. "Oh, *that* depot. Well, of course." She put her sandwich down and grabbed her napkin. Her hands shook. "I'm sorry. My mind was somewhere else. I would love to hear more stories from the depot. I know only my grandma's stories. Tell me some of Pinky's."

Kate crossed her arms. "Well, Gigi Pinky said it was the most wonderful time of her life. She said if she never accomplished anything else in her life, that was enough." Kate shrugged. "She met Great-Grandpa Abram there too. He was from Chicago."

"Was it love at first sight?" Carly asked.

"Gross." Chad made a horrible noise and pretended to gag. "Do we have to talk about mushy stuff?"

"Hush, Chad," Aunt Susie said. "You're outnumbered by girls."

Chad rolled his eyes and looked at Max for backup. Max stifled a laugh.

"I don't think so," Kate said. "I think Gigi thought he seemed nice and wanted to do something to encourage him. Great-Grandpa gave her his address, so she wrote."

Shelly sighed. "What a wonderful story. Thank you for sharing it with me."

Kate's eyes narrowed, and Max knew exactly what was going through her mind. Shelly should have known that story.

CHAPTER 10

Noise in the Alley

KATE TURNED ON THE BEDSIDE lamp in her upstairs bedroom and flipped off the overhead light. It was almost dark outside. She looked at her alarm clock. Eight o'clock. The Johnsons would be in church since it was Wednesday. Sometimes she went to church with them, but not tonight. She was tired.

Kate watched the curtain blow in the breeze. She took a deep breath of cool evening air and felt the tension drain from her shoulders. She got that from her mom. Mom had always wanted to open the windows as soon as it was warm enough, which was always before Dad thought it was. She giggled. Kate slept with her window open except on the coldest nights in the winter. Dad said he guessed it was okay since she slept upstairs and no one could get in the window from outside, but he still fixed the window so it opened only a few inches.

Kate heard footsteps on the gravel in the alley. She hurried to the window. *Maybe it's the Johnsons.* She glanced at the clock again, and frowned. *It's still early. Since Carly's dad is the pastor, he has to lock up. But maybe it's Slim and Earl?* She peered out the window. *What on earth?* She stepped back out of sight. *What's*

94

she doing there? Kate peeked around the curtain again to see if she had really seen right. Yep, it was Shelly—and the gate to the Johnson's backyard was swinging back and forth. *That latch never did work well.* Kate shook her head. She couldn't think of a single good reason why Shelly would be in the Johnson's backyard. *Carly and Max need to know this.*

Kate picked up the family picture she kept on her bedside table and pretended to be her mother. "Now Kate, don't jump to conclusions. You need a good night's sleep. All of this excitement has you plumb tired out. Deal with it in the morning." Kate smiled at the picture. "Thanks, Mom," she whispered. She grabbed her library book and climbed in bed. *I'll read until I'm sleepy. Mom's right. All of this drama is exhausting.*

The next morning Kate hurried into the kitchen and grabbed a bowl out of the cupboard, then poured cereal into it. As she reached into the fridge for the milk, she heard a knock at the front door.

"I'll get it," her dad called.

Kate poured her milk, then put it back in the fridge. *Who could that be?* She glanced down the hall and stopped in her tracks. There in their entryway were Slim, Earl, and Carly's dad.

Kate ducked out of sight. *What are they doing here?* She eased the door open between the kitchen and the dining room. Since the dining room led into the living room, she should be able to hear what was going on. She slid down on the floor by the door and took a bite of cereal.

"What brings you guys here?" Kate heard her dad ask.

There was silence. Finally Slim spoke. "Well, I don't know where to start so I'll just spit it out. Earl found this in the pocket of his jacket this morning."

More silence. Kate stopped chewing. *What was it?* She wished she had elastic eyes that could go around doors.

"Is this the money?" Nate asked.

"It appears so, Sir," Slim said. "There's four hundred and thirty dollars in there, and it looks like the envelope we saw on the coffee table. But—"

Earl cut Slim off. "I don't know how it got in my coat. Honest, Dr. Nate! I didn't take it, I promise. I haven't worn that jacket for a couple days, it's been so warm. I never stole nothing in my life, and I sure ain't startin' now." He sounded desperate. "I didn't know what to do. I was afraid to bring it over 'cause I know how it looks. But if I keep it, then I *am* guilty. So, there it is."

Silence again. Kate watched her Cheerios floating in the milk. She believed him—but why? All of a sudden, the noise outside her window the night before flew through her mind. Shelly.

Kate got to her feet, set her bowl on the dining room table, and started toward the living room. She had to tell him. Her dad's voice stopped her.

"Well. It's hard to believe you, Earl. But, I'm thankful you returned it. Real thankful."

Carly's dad cleared his throat. "It is hard to know what's what. But I agree with Dr. Nate that it's a good thing you two did, bringing it over here."

"I think we need to call this a closed case," Kate's dad said. "But I really don't want you around my office, Earl. I don't know what to think."

"I understand, sir. I know how it looks. Thank you for not calling the cops. They sure wouldn't have believed me. I won't bother you. As soon as I can get my pickup fixed, I'll be out of here." He sounded discouraged and kind of mad.

Kate heard the men get up.

"We better get to work," Slim said. "We're already a few minutes late, but we knew we had to take care of this right away."

"Well, thanks," her dad said. Kate heard him follow the men to the door, and the door clicked shut.

Kate slipped into the hall. Her dad leaned on the door with one hand, the other behind his head.

"Dad?"

He looked up. "I guess you heard that?"

She nodded.

"Do you believe him?"

Kate bit her lip. "It doesn't make sense. Why would he bring it back if he took it?"

Her dad nodded. "I know. But how else would the money get in his pocket?"

"Well . . . " Kate looked at her feet.

Her dad crossed the hall and tipped her chin up. "Do you have something to say?"

Tears welled in her eyes, and she nodded. "Can we sit down?"

Her dad grabbed her hand and squeezed. He led her into the living room and sat on the couch. "Okay, tell me about it."

"Last night, just before dark, I heard something outside my window." Kate took a deep breath to steady her nerves. "When I looked out, I saw Shelly leaving the Johnson's backyard. I thought it was kind of strange, but figured she was looking for them or something. But when Earl said the money was in his pocket but he didn't take it . . . "

Her dad tipped his head sideways. "Kate, you think Shelly took the money? I know you didn't get off to a good start with her, but do you really think she would steal it and frame someone else?" He shook his head. "That makes even less sense than Earl taking it."

Kate studied her hands. "I know."

Her dad leaned back and rubbed his eyes with his hand. "Honey, I think we need to put this behind us and start over with Shelly, okay?"

Kate's heart sank. "I'll try. But . . . can Carly and the other kids come help at the apartment again today? I want to like Shelly, but she makes me nervous. The other day, after the money disappeared, she was really angry."

Her dad's eyes narrowed. "What do you mean, angry? She didn't touch you, did she?"

Kate shook her head vehemently. "Oh no, nothing like that. But she hollered and used some awful language and went on and on. Yesterday she was nice." She sighed. "I want to like her. She is mom's cousin and friend . . . but I'll feel better if I have my friends and their Aunt Susie around."

Her dad nodded. "That's not a bad idea. Besides, you kids were making great progress on the place. I'll take the pickup today, and we can put a bunch of those boxes in the back and bring them home tonight." He slapped his legs. "Okay. Let's get going. I'll call Pastor Jeff and see if they can help this morning. I sure would like to get the apartment cleaned out soon."

The cousins sat in Aunt Susie's SUV, waiting. "Go ahead and get in. I'll be back in a minute," Aunt Susie had said as they piled into her vehicle. "I want to talk to Jeff."

"I don't get it." Max pulled the seatbelt across him. He turned around from the front passenger seat and looked at Carly. "It makes no sense that Earl would take the money and then give it back like that."

Carly shook her head. "I know. You would think he would have taken off."

"But Daddy thinks he did it," Molly said.

"How do you know that?" Max asked. "He didn't say that at breakfast."

"I know," Molly said. "But when I came down the stairs a few minutes ago, I was practicing walking right next to the wall so the steps wouldn't squeak, and I heard Mom and Dad in the hall. I stopped. I didn't mean to listen, but I was stuck. I couldn't go down, and I was afraid to go back up or they might hear me."

"What did they say?" Chad leaned forward from the back seat.

"Well, Dad said that as much as he wanted to believe Earl, the evidence was overwhelming." Molly wrinkled up her forehead. "I think that's how he said it."

"It really does look bad," Max agreed.

"But then Dad said Slim had one-hundred percent confidence in Earl, and Slim got upset with Dad 'cause he could tell he didn't believe Earl." Molly's voice faded until it was hardly above a whisper. "Mom said she hoped this didn't make Slim so upset he would leave."

"No!" Chad hollered.

Max flinched. *This is terrible. We have to do something.*

CHAPTER 11

The Long View

"CARLY, CAN YOU AND MAX help me carry these boxes out to Dad's pickup?" Kate held a key ring. "Dad gave me his keys." She giggled. "He told me not to go crazy and run all over town."

"Why do we need the keys?" Carly shut the box of photo albums she had just finished packing, and Max taped it shut. Carly took the marker and wrote the words "Photo Albums" on the box.

Kate rattled the keys in her hand. "The pickup cap has a lock. We'll need the keys to get it open. Dad wants us to load these and some of the boxes from the storage room into the pickup to take home."

Max nodded. "Sure, we'll help. Let's go."

Carly poked her head into the bathroom where her aunt was cleaning out the closet and packing the towels—all pink, of course. "We're going downstairs to load boxes into Dr. Nate's pickup."

"Who's we?" Aunt Susie asked.

"Max, Kate, and me," Carly said. "I guess names would be helpful."

"Sounds good." Aunt Susie turned away, but not before Carly noticed her red eyes. She had been crying. She was upset when she came out of the house after talking to Dad. Now she was upset again. Or still. Carly wanted to run in and give Aunt Susie a big hug, but she followed Max and Kate down the stairs.

Just as Kate reached the bottom step, the outside door opened and Shelly rushed in. "Hi, guys! Sorry I'm late. What are you up to?"

Kate stiffened. "We're loading boxes into Dad's pickup."

"Ah, I wondered why he parked in the alley." Shelly squeezed Kate's shoulder as she passed her on the stairs. "I'll get up there and see how I can help."

Kate shrugged her shoulder and shoved the door open. "Let's get the pickup open first, and then we can start hauling boxes."

Out in the alley, Kate unlocked and opened the cap.

"It sure is nice this is a covered alley," Carly said. "Even if it rained, you could load stuff out here."

Kate nodded. "It is nice. Gigi Pinky loved it. She could walk right across the street to the diner and barely be in the weather."

Max pulled up the handle and lowered the tailgate. "There." Max rubbed his hands on his jeans. "Now we're ready."

"Wait a minute." Kate hesitated, twirling the keys on her hand. "I want to tell you guys something." She dropped her voice and stepped closer to the cousins.

"What's up?" Carly asked.

"I saw something last night, and I don't know what to do about it. I told my dad, but he doesn't think it's important." She shuddered. "I thought maybe you could help."

"What did you see?" Carly asked.

Kate rocked back and forth from one foot to the other. "I saw Shelly come out of your backyard while you were all at church. Why would she be there?" She stopped. "I didn't think too much of it at the time, but when Earl came over with the money and insisted—" she swallowed hard, "insisted he didn't take the money—" Kate closed her eyes and shook her head. "I couldn't help but wonder about Shelly. What if she . . . " Her voice trailed away.

Carly gasped. "But why? Why would she do that to Earl?"

Kate shook her head. "I have no idea. I was hoping you would. Dad just thinks Shelly and I got off to a bad start, but I told him how angry she was the other day, and he didn't like that." Kate raced on, the words spilling out like someone had opened a fire hydrant. "I told him I didn't want to be by myself with her, and he said you could come." She stopped and a tiny smile appeared on her tense face. "I think he called her when we got here. I heard him on the phone, and he sounded really firm. I heard him say he wanted to hear only positive things from his daughter about her day. He also said the money is a closed topic now. He didn't want to hear any opinions from her." Kate stood up straighter. "I was surprised, 'cause Dad's kind of an easygoing guy. I felt like he was sticking up for me."

"Whew," Max said. "I don't know what to think. That's a lot to process."

"I know. Thanks for listening," Kate said. "I'm not sure what we would do about it anyway, but I feel better now that you know." Kate hurried to the door. "Dad will be glad when we get this pickup loaded. We want only the boxes going to the house in this load. Then we can bring the boxes headed to the Salvation Army downstairs and put them in with the others."

"That will make a big dent in what's still up there," Carly said. "We haven't even touched the pictures on the walls, though. And that coin. What about the coin?"

"I'll have to ask Dad." Kate hurried into the storage room and lifted a box. "We'll sure get our exercise."

"Yeah, and our *mental* exercise, figuring out what's up with Shelly," Max said.

By noon the apartment looked bare, and the rooms echoed whenever anyone walked through them. All of the closets were empty except for the stacked boxes, waiting to be hauled away. The cabinets in the bathroom and kitchen were bare. The cleaning supplies and paper products sat on one end of the kitchen counter. The knickknacks on the furniture had been examined for hidden spots in an effort to find the necklace before being packed away. Carly could smell bleach. Aunt Susie had even scrubbed the tub in the bathroom, trying to remove old lime deposits.

"Hey, maybe we should look in that clock." Max pointed to the brown clock that chimed the hour. "Remember the hidden compartment in Miss Belle's clock?"

"What a good idea!" Carly said. She turned to Shelly, who was sorting through the papers from the buffet drawer. "Could you please lift that clock down from the china cabinet? We had a friend who had a secret compartment in her clock."

Shelly hurried over to the clock, lifted it down, and placed it on the table. "It's worth a try. That necklace has to be here somewhere."

They all gathered around the clock. "Where should we start?" Shelly ran her fingers over the wood.

"Can I?" Max stepped up to the clock.

"Go ahead," Shelly said. She held her hands up and backed away. "I don't have the first idea where to look."

"Well, it was about here, wasn't it, Carly?" Max tugged at the side of the clock.

Carly nodded. "I think so."

She watched as Max pushed and pulled, tapped and jiggled the beautiful smooth wood. Finally he threw up his hands. "I guess this clock doesn't have one."

"It was a good idea," Kate said. She smiled at Max. "Don't worry. We'll find it, I know we will."

"I hope it's soon," Shelly muttered.

Carly looked over at the woman and caught her breath. *Oh boy, crabby Shelly is back.*

Carly saw Aunt Susie's eyes narrow. She stood up abruptly and grabbed her jacket. "Well, kids, it's about lunch time. I think you are expected at home for lunch today. We'll have to come over tomorrow and help some more." She looked around the room. "I think tomorrow we should be able to get the last bits packed up. Then all that will be left is the furniture."

Kate stepped closer to Carly. "What are you doing this afternoon? Can I come?"

Carly glanced at Shelly.

"I have plans this afternoon," Shelly said. "Whatever you do will have to be without me."

Carly saw Kate relax. "Come home with us if it's okay with your dad."

Kate hurried to the door. "I'll go ask him."

Carly and Kate were elated when Carly's parents agreed that the kids could go to the Golden Spike Tower. Carly gave Kate a high five. "I've wanted to see that for a long time."

"Me too," Kate said. "Everyone in my class at school has been there but me. It sounds so cool. We hear about the railroad and how important it is here in town, how many tracks there are, and the historic stuff about it, but all I ever see or hear are the trains going by two blocks from our house every few minutes. As far as I know, there's only one track. I don't even notice the horn anymore."

"Do you feel your house rattle when the train goes by?" Chad asked.

Kate nodded. "Yeah, but I hardly notice that either."

Carly's dad laughed. "You'll know there are more than one track after you go to the Golden Spike. Sure wish I could go too."

The doorbell rang and Carly jumped, dropping her fork. The front door opened and a voice called, "Anyone home?"

Carly couldn't believe her eyes. "Brandon! What are you doing here?"

"And how did you get here?" Carly's mom asked. "I know you didn't walk."

Great-Uncle Floyd, Grandpa Johnson's brother, popped his head through the doorway behind Brandon. "Are we too late for lunch?"

Max jumped up from the table and dashed over to Brandon. The cousins, only a few months apart in age, smacked each other on the back. Chad headed for the office. "I'll get chairs."

Within a couple of moments, two more chairs had been pulled up and plates and silverware obtained from the kitchen.

"I thought you couldn't come until tomorrow," Carly said. She handed the plate of sloppy joes to Brandon.

"That's right, but when Uncle Floyd stopped, heading this way, I talked Mom and Dad into letting me come a day early. Mom thought we should call, but Dad said you wouldn't mind, and he thought it would be fun to surprise you." Brandon gave Uncle Floyd a thumbs-up. "And we did, didn't we?"

Two hours later, the cousins, Kate, Aunt Susie, and Carly's mom nibbled on the sample fudge being offered free at the Golden Spike and then waited as the elevator took them to the top of the tower. They had already seen the video describing Bailey Yard, the largest rail yard in the world. Now, they were on their way to the top to see it for themselves. Max, backed into the corner next to Kate and Carly, leaned against the wall and thought about the mystery. After lunch, while Carly's parents and Aunt Susie visited with Uncle Floyd, the cousins had given Brandon a rundown of the events of the week. He had been horrified that Shelly accused Slim, but he wasn't convinced Earl was innocent or Shelly guilty.

Max tried to put thoughts of Earl and Shelly out of his mind. He was ready to have some fun. But, every time he thought of that Shelly woman, his stomach tensed.

The elevator stopped with a gentle jerk, and the doors slid open. Chad dashed out and the others followed. Max stopped and looked around. *Wow! This is impressive.* He followed Carly to the window overlooking the railroad yard. Carly gasped. "Daddy was right. There *is* more than one train track."

No matter which direction Max looked, he saw tracks and train cars that were being shuttled in several different directions. Trains moved both east and west. There were a few people, small as toys in a playroom. It was like looking down on an intricate train set. The sounds of the train yard were muffled by distance and the windows, but Max could still hear the roar of big engines and the sound of train wheels rumbling over the rails.

"Hey, Max!" Chad hollered from across the tower. "Look at this. It's a binocular thing!" Chad stood beside a tourist telescope positioned so onlookers could get a closer view of what was happening below. "It costs only a quarter," he said.

Max fished in his pocket while he hurried across the platform. "I think I have a couple of quarters, Chad. I'll put one in, and we can split the time, okay?"

Chad climbed up on the step and pointed to the spot for the coins. "You put the money there."

"I see that." Max rolled his eyes at Brandon. Once the money was inserted, Max looked through the scope and focused it. "This is cool," he said. "You can see what's going on down there up close and personal. I can see guys working and everything! It's incredible."

"Let me look, let me look!" Chad bounced around the telescope.

Max backed down and held his hand out. "Okay! Hurry up."

Chad held tight to the scope and peered through it. Max waited beside him and looked down. So many trains. It was hard to believe this constant motion happened around the clock right outside North Platte.

Chad whooped and hollered. "I can see it all from here!" He swung the telescope over to the right. "I want to look over here." He peered through the scope again. All of a sudden he shrieked. "Hey, I see Earl! And—" He gasped. "It's Slim." He turned his head and stared at Max. "It's Earl and Slim."

"No it isn't," Max said. "Why would they be out here?"

Chad stuck his chin out. "You look then."

Max moved up to the scope and pushed his eyes up to the glass. It *was* Slim and Earl. They looked like they were arguing. Suddenly, the scope went dark. "Argh! It needs more money." His hands shook as he dug the coin out of his pocket and put it into the machine. He turned to Carly, Kate, and Brandon. "He's right. It's Slim and Earl." He leaned back into the machine and looked again, his hands gripping the cold metal telescope. It took him a few seconds to find them. They were bent over, hiding behind a train car. Slim waved his arms.

"What can you see?" Carly grabbed Max's arm.

"Oh, no, no, no!" Max's voice got louder with each *no* until it was an anguished shriek. He lifted his head from the scope and stared at the other kids.

"What's wrong, Max?" Carly's mom asked. "You're white as a sheet." She and Aunt Susie had heard him cry out and had hurried over.

Max swallowed hard. He opened his mouth, but no words came out. He closed his eyes and shuddered. Then he croaked out the words blasting around in his brain. "I just saw Earl and Slim sneak onto an empty car. They're leaving on that train." He turned to the window and pointed to a train, slowly moving to the west.

CHAPTER 12

"Trust but Verify"

EXCEPT FOR FREQUENT SNIFFLES, THE ride back to the house was silent. Aunt Susie stared straight ahead as she drove. She parked the car in her usual spot, and everyone climbed out. Carly followed the rest of the kids as they dragged themselves toward the house. Carly felt like they were moving in slow motion while her mind raced so fast it threatened to explode. A lump settled in her stomach, and she couldn't seem to get a deep breath. When she got to the front door, Carly glanced back at the vehicle. Aunt Susie still sat in the driver's seat, her head down.

"Are you absolutely sure it was Slim and Earl?" Carly's dad shoved his hand through his hair. "I simply don't believe Slim would take off that way. I don't believe it," he repeated. The cousins and Kate huddled together on the couch and piano bench. Carly held her head in her hand and felt the tears drip through her fingers. She tasted salt on her lips.

"I'm ninety-nine percent sure," Max said, his voice shaking. "Slim had his favorite Denver Broncos shirt on—and Earl had on that blue shirt he wears most of the time."

The front door opened, and Aunt Susie came in from the car. The others all looked up at her. She was still pale, but she had a weak smile on her face. "I texted Slim and asked if everything was okay."

"And?" Carly's dad asked, his eyebrows raised.

"He responded with one word: *Later.*" Susie lifted Chad up off the couch, settled next to Max, and held Chad close. "That usually means he's in the middle of something and will get back to me."

"Like leaving town on a train," Max said, head in his hands.

Aunt Susie stretched her head side to side. "I'm sure there's an explanation if it was Slim and Earl you saw. I trust him. If he says he'll tell me later, he will. You all trust him too, don't you?"

A weak chorus of "yesses" arose around the room. Carly brushed the tears from her face and sat up. *Yes, she trusted Slim.* A flutter of hope rose in her heart.

"Absolutely!" Carly's dad blew his breath out. "He told Earl the other night he was finished with that life, and I believe him. We'll have to wait for him to come home and explain what you saw, Max."

"You trust Slim like he trusts Earl," Kate said. "Pastor Johnson, I don't know how the money got into Earl's pocket, but I believe him. I don't think he did it."

Carly held her breath. What Kate said made sense. They trusted Slim enough to wait for him to explain. When she thought of it that way, she understood why Slim was so certain Earl was innocent. She squeezed Kate's hand.

"Ah, Kate. You are right. But, I guess I'm thinking like President Reagan did back in the 1980s," Carly's dad said. "Do any of you know what he said to Russian President Gorbachev at one of their meetings?"

"Is that the Reagan quote you always use?" Molly asked.

Her dad grinned. "Hmmm. Do I use it that much?"

Carly, Molly, and their mom all answered together. "Yes!" Then Molly leaned forward and gave her best imitation of her dad's voice. "Trust, but verify!"

"That's it! I do trust Slim, and I know he is absolutely convinced Earl did not steal the money," Carly's dad said. "I want to believe it, but I have no way to prove it. So, until I do, I can't say with one-hundred percent certainty that he isn't guilty. But neither will I treat him like a thief. Does that make sense?"

Kate nodded. "Well, I hope we figure it out soon. I hate not knowing what happened," she said.

The house phone rang. "I'll get it," Carly's dad stood up. He paused in the doorway to the dining room. "I would suggest you kids find something to do. I have an idea. Let me get this call and I'll tell you." He hurried to the phone and answered.

Carly leaned back against the piano keys. *Dad probably has a work project in mind. He's just like Grandpa Johnson. If you are fretting about something, his idea of a good cure is work, and as much as I hate to admit it, he's usually right.*

Her dad's voice interrupted her thoughts.

"Sutherland? You're over in Sutherland?" her dad said into the phone. "No, no problem. Give me a few minutes and I'll be there . . . uh-huh . . . yeah, the kids saw you from the tower. Caused quite a stir here."

All of the kids jumped to their feet. "It's Slim." Chad kept his voice low.

Carly held her breath, straining to hear every word her dad said.

"Yeah, they were all pretty shook up, but we decided to trust you. Well, let me get off here, and I'll be over to pick you guys up . . . uh-huh . . . At what café? . . . I've got it. See you in a few."

Before he even got the phone back on its base, the kids had surrounded Carly's dad, all of them talking at once. "What happened? That was Slim, wasn't it?"

A huge grin split her dad's face. "Yep, it was Slim. You did see them jump a train, Max, but they both got off at Sutherland. I'm going over now to pick them up." He held his hand up. "No, I don't know any more than that. And no, you can't go with me. He asked me to come alone. He and Earl need to talk to me first." He turned to Aunt Susie. "He did tell me he will call you in a couple of minutes."

"Hurray!" Chad started bouncing, and he bounced from the dining room clear to the rear of the house and back to the front.

Carly felt like she would explode from relief and nervous energy. "Dad, you were going to tell us something we can do. I can't believe I'm asking for work, but I need something to do."

Her dad laughed. "I know what you mean, Carly. I thought you could start clearing out the flower beds along the fence. I notice there are flowers starting to poke through the leaves. It needs done. You can put the leaves in those brown bags we keep in the garage."

"Oh, can I help?" Kate asked. "I love yard work," she said. "Hey, I could call my dad, and ask if we can do ours too when we're done here!"

Carly's dad kissed his wife and headed for the door. "Sounds good to me. If you all work together, I bet you can get all the flower beds in both yards done in the next couple of hours." To his wife he said, "Don't expect me until supper time, Sheila. I'm going to spend some time with our two train jumpers."

Max bounced up off the chair by the door. "Let's do it!"

Carly pulled her hand back from the rake and let the wet leaves drop into the large brown bag Molly held open for her. She shook the rake to remove the leaves that wanted to stick. Her back ached, but boy, did it feel good to be outside and working. The frantic thoughts in her mind had settled as they cleaned out the flower beds in her yard and then the ones at Kate's. She leaned on her rake for a minute as Molly closed the bag, now full of leaves, sticks, and other debris. The smell of damp cold dirt, covered all winter by the leaves, made Carly thankful spring was here. The daffodils, hyacinths, and lilies of the valley were already poking their heads up above ground. Like Kate, Carly loved working in dirt.

Kate and Max laughed at Chad's antics. He was supposed to be holding the bag for them, but he darted around like a linebacker in a football game, and the bag became a moving target. Kate, her face flushed, threw her head back and laughed. Carly pushed her hair back off her forehead, then frowned as she felt the mud smear on her face. *Oh, I bet I'm a sight!*

"Hello!" The Johnson's back gate squeaked open. Slim and Earl stood in the opening. Slim, fists on his hips, called across the alley. "I've been told I should notify you that supper will be ready in thirty minutes, but I don't suppose you're hungry."

Carly dropped her rake and raced toward Slim, but Max and Chad outran her. Before you could say *supercalifragilisticexpialidocious*, the two men were mobbed by the cousins and Kate.

Chad launched himself into Slim's arms and hung on as if his very life depended on it. Huge sobs exploded from the boy. Max shook Earl's hand as hard as he could, then turned to Slim. Molly leaned on Slim's arm. Carly, Brandon, and Kate hovered in front of them, grinning from ear to ear. Max put his finger in Slim's face. "You scared us to death, Slim! It was horrible."

Whoa! Carly's mouth flew open. Max looked mad, but he also looked like he wanted to throw his arms around Slim and cry just like Chad.

"I thought I might never see you again," Chad mumbled into Slim's neck.

Slim cleared his throat. He patted Chad's back a few times, then set him down and pulled Max in for a hug. "I'm sorry, guys. I never dreamed you would see me there. How crazy is that?" He shook his head, then went around the group, one at a time, looking each of them in the eye. "I never planned to leave. I was trying to talk Earl into staying. I was pretty determined." He grinned at his friend. "I won."

Carly smiled at Earl. "We're glad you came back."

Slim cleared his throat again. "I can't say though that the temptation to jump a train hasn't reared its head since I met you, but something stops me every time."

"What's that?" Brandon asked.

"Knowing that you trust me and depend on me to stay on course." Slim swallowed hard. "Your trust in me gives me the accountability I need to help me say, 'No Thanks!' when the temptation arises."

"And Aunt Susie," Chad said. He dried his eyes on his sleeve. "You like Aunt Susie, don't you?"

Earl snorted. Max rolled his eyes. "Chad Rawson! You know Mom says not to say stuff like that."

"What?" Chad stuck his chin out. "I'm not stupid. I can tell when people like each other, and Slim and Aunt Susie like each other."

Slim turned beet red. "Yes, Chad. I do care a lot for Susie. But right now I'm talking about you guys, okay?"

"Okay," Chad said. He glared at Max. "See, I was right."

"So, getting back to what I was saying," Slim said. "I promise I won't leave. With God's help and your love, I'll still be here when you are old."

"But, Slim," Chad said, his face wrinkled with concern, "when we're old, you'll be . . . well, dead."

Earl laughed so hard he choked, and his laughter was so contagious, the others couldn't keep from laughing with him. Carly felt herself relax. It felt so good to laugh.

Kate sidled up to Earl. She pulled herself up to her full height, and her jaw jutted out. "Mr. Earl, I have something to say."

Earl wiped the tears of laughter from his eyes. "What is it, little lady?"

"I want you to know that I believe you. I know you didn't take the money. I know some people don't believe you, but I wanted you to know I do," Kate said.

Earl's mouth dropped open, and he ducked his head and shuffled his feet. "Thank you. That means a lot to me."

A car horn honked, and Carly saw Dr. Nate pull into their driveway. Kate waved to her dad before turning to her friends. "Bye, guys, I have to go! I need to get out of these clothes. Thursday night is date night at our house." She wrinkled up her nose. "I don't think Dad will want to take me to Merrick's in these muddy jeans. I'll see you in the morning. There's a burger basket with my name on it! I'm famished."

The next morning Carly glanced out the window on the stairwell, and what she saw stopped her in her tracks. Kate was flying across the back yard, and the look on her face wasn't a happy one. She looked terrified.

Carly raced back down the stairs, through the hall, and into the kitchen. She pushed open the back door just as Kate reached for the door knob. "What's wrong?" She searched Kate's face for a hint. Kate bent over, gasping for breath.

"Look at this!" She held out an envelope and a rumpled letter with a trembling hand.

Carly took the envelope and the letter. It was the one she had found under the jewelry box a few days earlier. "It's the letter from Shelly."

Kate took a deep breath. "Yeah, from the real Shelly." She dropped her voice to a whisper. "I don't know who *this* Shelly is, but I don't believe for a minute she's my mother's cousin."

Carly's mouth dropped open, but Kate continued. "We need to get the others and talk. I asked Dad if I can ride in to the office with you guys. We need a plan." She grabbed Carly's hand and squeezed until it hurt.

Carly's mind was a muddled whirl. "They're all upstairs. We were brushing our teeth and making our beds before Aunt Susie gets here."

"Well, they better brush fast. This is an emergency."

CHAPTER 13

Imposter

Two minutes later the kids had gathered in the play room. Carly pulled Kate down beside her. Kate shook so hard her teeth chattered.

"What's the big deal?" Chad asked. He still had toothpaste on his face. "I wasn't even done brushing when Max dragged me out of the bathroom."

Kate nodded at the letter in Carly's hand. "Carly found this in Gigi Pinky's bedroom under her jewelry box. It's from Shelly to Gigi. It was written a year ago this month." Her voice dropped. "She said she was on her annual buying trip to Europe." She swallowed hard. "Carly, could you please read it out loud? I'm so upset, I can't even talk."

Carly started to read.

Dear Aunt Pinky,

I hope you are well. I am writing from Paris where I'm halfway through my annual buying trip. You know how it is every March and April.

Yesterday, while poking around an antique store, I found a treasure. It reminded me of you and Kathy. Tucked in the back of a tiny shop, I found a life-sized statue of a Native American man. I instantly found myself back at the top of Sioux Lookout, staring at the big Indian statue with you, Kathy, and Grandma Pepper. What wonderful times we had! Sioux Lookout was by far my favorite place of all the places you took us. Did you know that when Kathy and I carved our names in the hill at Sioux Lookout, we promised we would return when we turned the awful old age of forty? I'll be forty soon; guess I should come out to visit and take Kate up to find her mother's name.

I couldn't help but remember that this month marks the first anniversary of Kathy's death. I was in Europe then too. I still regret not coming home for the service.

I wanted you to know how honored I am that you entrusted me with the care of the Buffalo Bill necklace. I fully approve of your hiding place. Be assured I will make certain it's properly protected, cared for, and passed on when you are gone.

If you ever need to contact me, here's my phone number. It works no matter where I am.

"And then there's a phone number," Carly said. A cold chill went through Carly, and she could feel the goose bumps on her arms. She dropped the letter in her lap and rubbed them. Now she understood the fear in Shelly's eyes.

"I don't think the Shelly here is really Shelly," Kate whispered. "I think Shelly is in Europe on her annual buying trip. Shelly should know exactly where the necklace is. If she is Shelly, why would she act like she doesn't know?"

Carly stabbed her finger at the letter. "This Shelly sounds like she loved your Gigi and your mom very much."

"Did you show it to your dad?" Brandon asked.

Kate shook her head firmly and bit her lip. "When I told him that I saw Shelly come out of your yard Wednesday night, he didn't believe me. He keeps telling me I'm misunderstanding her and I need to try to get to know her better. I need absolute proof."

"How are we going to get that?" Molly scooted clear back into the corner of the room. "We can't ask her if she is really Shelly. And we sure don't want to make her feel threatened."

"That's why I need your help. You're the detectives." Kate looked around at each of them, her eyes pleading. "You have to help me."

"You could call the number," Max suggested. "If Fake Shelly answers, you know she is probably legit."

"And if not?" Carly asked.

"The other day she said her favorite place was Buffalo Bill's house," Molly said. "But in the letter she definitely said she loves Sioux Lookout best."

"Well, even if she comes out here, the warrior isn't there anymore," Kate said.

"Why not?" Max asked. "Where did it go?"

"So many people vandalized it by using it for target practice that they moved it into town. It's on the corner by the Courthouse," Molly said.

"Oh no," Chad said. He slapped his hand over his face.

"We could mention Sioux Lookout and see what Shelly says." Brandon flipped a toy soldier over and over in his hand. "Even if she doesn't always think of it as her favorite, she would know what it is."

Kate's eyes lit up. "Those are both great ideas. I knew you guys would be able to help!"

"Kids, are you ready?" Carly's mom's voice drifted up the stairs and across the house. "Aunt Susie is here."

"One more thing," Carly said. "After we do our two tests, if she isn't really Shelly we have to go downstairs to the office and tell your dad. We can't confront her without him."

"Carly's right," Max said. "That would be too dangerous, and we don't want dangerous. Either you agree to that, or we need to tell Carly's parents before we go."

Kate squirmed. "I don't want to tell any of the grown-ups until we're absolutely sure. What if we're wrong?" Kate asked. "But I don't want dangerous either. I promise."

Once at the apartment, Carly felt Kate nudge her. She took a deep breath. "Aunt Susie, can Kate borrow your phone? She needs to make a quick call."

Aunt Susie pulled her phone out of her pocket. "Sure, here you go, sweetie." She handed it to Kate, then looked at the living room walls. "I guess we've avoided this as long as we can. I'm going to pull the pictures and framed artifacts down. We can pack them up and send them to your house for your grandma to decide what she wants to do."

Kate and Carly hurried back to Pinky's office in the little room next to the bedroom. Kate pulled out the letter. She took a deep breath and punched the number into the cell phone. "Here we go."

The girls put their heads together. Carly held her breath while the phone rang. Finally, after five rings a voice came on. It was voice mail. Carly stiffened. This was not Fake Shelly's voice. This voice sounded higher. And it wasn't gravelly. When the phone beeped, Kate tried to talk, but nothing came out. She cleared her throat and started again. "Hi, Shelly. This is Kate Neilson, Kathy's daughter. It's really important for you to call my dad, Nate. Here is his number." She recited her dad's number. "Please call as soon as you can. It's really, *really* important. Uh, kind of an emergency. Thanks. Bye."

Kate ended the call and stared at Carly. "That wasn't Fake Shelly."

"No," Carly said. "It wasn't." Carly thought she was going to throw up.

"Hi there!" Fake Shelly's voice rang out through the apartment.

Carly jumped. "Oh, boy. Time for step two."

Kate's jaw jutted out again. "It's time to stop this big fat liar in her tracks."

Carly grabbed Kate's arm. "Remember, you promised we'll go get your dad if she fails step two. There's no telling what she'll do when she's confronted."

Kate pulled her arm away. "I know, I know. Let's go."

When the two girls came into the living room, Max, Brandon, and Molly were pulling frames off the walls. "Look at this, Carly." Max walked over and held out the frame with the article about the depot. "I bet you'll want to read this one." He turned his back on Aunt Susie and Fake Shelly and raised his eyebrows in a silent question.

"Step two," Carly whispered. She plastered a smile on her face. "This is great, Max. I would love to read this entire article."

Kate put Aunt Susie's phone down on the empty bookshelf by the buffet. "Hey, guys. I know of a great place to visit this afternoon."

Molly looked like she was about to faint, but she asked the question she had been assigned earlier. "Where?" Her voice, a bit wobbly, floated across the room.

"Sioux Lookout," Kate said. She tossed her hair. "It's a great climb."

"Can you still go up there?" Carly asked.

"What is Sioux Lookout?" Fake Shelly asked. She stood between the couch and the buffet, hands on her hips.

Carly's heart beat so hard she was sure Fake Shelly could see it, and her legs felt like jelly. She looked at Kate, and she knew they were in trouble. Kate's face had gone completely still and very pale. Her jaw was stuck out farther than Carly had ever seen it, and her eyes burned holes right into Fake Shelly.

"Um, it's the highest point in the area, and it's where Native Americans would watch for their enemies," Carly said. "Kate, let's go check on that thing downstairs."

She grabbed Kate's arm, but Kate jerked away. She took a step toward Fake Shelly and then another. She glared at the woman. Through gritted teeth she spit out the words. "Who. Are. You?"

The woman's head jerked back as if she had been slapped, and she took a little step backwards. "What on earth?" Fake Shelly threw a look at Aunt Susie, who looked completely befuddled.

"Kate, what are you talking about?" Aunt Susie asked.

Kate never took her eyes off the imposter. "This woman is not Shelly. I don't know who she is, but she's not Shelly." She jerked the letter out of her pocket and waved it in the air. "This letter is from Shelly. This is the end of March, and Shelly always goes to Europe in March. In this letter, Shelly, the *real* Shelly, says that her favorite site was Sioux Lookout." Her voice rose until it was a shriek. "The place you don't even know about. I called the real Shelly, and her voice mail message sounds nothing like you." By now Kate stood toe to toe with Fake Shelly, who had backed up until her back was flat against the buffet. Kate lifted her finger and shook it in the woman's face. "So tell me. Who are you?"

Aunt Susie hurried around the couch, put her hands on Kate's shoulders, and pulled her back a couple of steps. Carly stepped up beside Kate. Max and Brandon were frozen in place, off to Fake Shelly's left, by the bookshelf. Molly crept up beside her aunt.

"Is this true?" Aunt Susie asked in a low voice.

"Oh, don't be ridiculous," the woman said. "Do I have to get my driver's license out for you?"

"I would like that very much," Aunt Susie said, her voice calm but firm. "Let me see it." She put her hand on Molly's shoulder. "Go down and get Dr. Nate, please."

Fake Shelly twisted around, jerked open the drawer of the buffet, reached in, and quickly swung back around. She held a gun, a pink gun. She waved it at the semi-circle surrounding her. "No one is going anywhere."

"Put that gun down," Aunt Susie commanded, her voice booming through the near-empty apartment.

Carly froze. Her mouth felt so dry she couldn't even swallow. Out of the corner of her eye, she saw Max reach up to the bookshelf. He slipped Aunt Susie's phone into his hand. Brandon saw him and stepped forward as Max stepped back, hiding behind Brandon.

Kate was unfazed by the gun. "That thing's not loaded. Gigi Pinky never kept it loaded."

"I noticed that yesterday too, but I also found the bullets in the office. So, do you want to bet me it isn't loaded now?"

Kate backed up against Aunt Susie. Carly shuddered. She could see Max frantically pushing buttons on Aunt Susie's phone. *If he can send a text or call 911 like we did that night in Rapid City—*

"What is it you want?" Molly asked, her voice so soft you could hardly hear it.

"What do I want?" the woman hissed. "I want that necklace and the coin. I know where to get the other coin, but the real value is in the letter and the necklace."

"How do you even know about it?" Kate demanded.

The woman waved the gun. "I guess I can tell you now. I'm going to shove you all in that little office in a minute and get out of here." She spotted Max with the phone. "Give me that!"

Max pushed a button on the phone and backed up.

"Give me that phone." She darted over to Max, wrenched the phone from his hand, threw it on the floor, and stomped on it. "There! Now back to my little story. You see, I work for Shelly." When she said the name, her face contorted like she had smelled something bad. "I take care of her mom; you know she is losing her mind. Dementia, they call it. Some days she thinks I'm Shelly 'cause we're about the same build and both have long, dark hair, so when that happens," she held her hands palms up and shrugged her shoulders, "what's a girl to do? She started talking one day about that necklace, and I knew I had to get it."

"But we don't know where it is," Molly insisted.

"The real Shelly does." Kate glared at the woman. "She said so in this letter. But only *she* knows, and she's not here, is she?"

"Don't push buttons, Kate," Aunt Susie murmured. "Look, I don't know who you are," she said firmly to Fake Shelly, "but please put that gun down and leave. You haven't done anything really serious yet."

"Enough," Fake Shelly said. "Go. All of you. Get into the office. I am not going to jail."

"Where's Chad?" Carly whispered to Max as they hurried down the hall ahead of the woman with the pink gun.

He shook his head. "I don't know. Aunt Susie sent him downstairs for more boxes. I hope he stays out of her way."

Once they were all crowded into the study, like sardines in a can, the imposter leered at them. "Get comfy. It will be a while before you get out." She pulled the door shut, and they heard the door lock from the outside.

Kate stomped her foot and pulled at her hair. "Why did Gigi have to be so stubborn? Dad tried and tried to get her to change the locks on these doors so they didn't use skeleton keys. Now we're trapped."

CHAPTER 14

Scout to the Rescue

CHAD CREPT UP THE STAIRS in the hall, holding the collapsed boxes over his head. He scanned the horizon in every direction, on alert for Sioux warriors. He had to get the mail through; and now that his pony had been shot out from under him, he would have to go on foot. He slipped up each step, silent and cautious, staying to the edges so they didn't creak. In an instant he was ripped out of his imaginary world by four words: "Put down that gun."

He jerked to a stop. *That's Aunt Susie's voice. Why would she say that? Aunt Susie must be playing a game. But, Aunt Susie?* Creeping to the top of the stairs, he set the boxes down and slipped into the kitchen. He heard voices in the living room. That Shelly woman was talking. Then Molly said something, but he couldn't hear her clearly. He peeked around the corner, and his eyes nearly jumped out of his head. That Shelly woman had her back to that big piece of furniture, while the rest of them stood around her in a half circle. That Shelly woman held a gun. A pink one. Movement to the right caught his eye. Max had a phone.

Chad jerked when Shelly leaped over and ripped the phone from Max. Then she threw it down and stomped on it! Chad gasped. He backed around the corner, dropped to his knees, and crept out the door. Without making a sound he slipped down the steps, moving as fast as he could. He had to get help, and now! She must not be the real Shelly, just like Kate thought. But what had happened to getting Dr. Nate? Well, he would do it.

Once down the stairs, he turned to the right and, abandoning all caution, tore through the storage rooms and tumbled out into the hallway by the window to the receptionist's office.

He pounded on the window and bounced up and down so she would see him better. *Hurry up, lady, hurry up, lady!*

The lady behind the window looked at him over her half-glasses and smiled. Moving slower than a snail, she approached the window and slid it back. "How can I help you, young man?"

"Dr. Nate! I need Dr. Nate. It's an emergency!" He croaked. His mouth felt like he had a wad of cotton in it. "Please, hurry! I need him now."

The lady pursed her lips. "I'm sorry, young man, but he's in with a patient. Do you want to sit in the waiting room?"

Chad thought he would explode. "This is an *emergency*. There's a woman with a gun. A p-p-pink g-gun." He was stuttering and could feel the tears coming. "She has them all! I need Dr. Nate. I need him n-n-now!"

The woman's face froze. "What on earth? Slow down, young man; what are you talking about?"

At that moment, Dr. Nate himself came out of a room down the hall. Chad saw him and turned toward him. He opened his mouth to call for help, but nothing came out. It was like a bad dream. Everything moved in slow motion.

Dr. Nate's phone rang. He answered it. He listened. He got a confused look on his face. He glanced up at the ceiling, and a look of horror flew across his face. At that instant, Chad unfroze.

"Help," he screamed at the top of his lungs. "That Shelly woman has a pink gun upstairs, and it's pointed at everyone. You have to help!"

Dr. Nate tore past Chad. "Call 9-1-1," he shouted as he flew past the receptionist, whose half-glasses fell off her face.

Chad dashed behind Dr. Nate through the hall, the storage rooms, and to the stairs. Just as they reached the bottom step, the back door flew open, and Slim and Earl almost collided with Dr. Nate.

"What are you doing here?" Dr. Nate asked. He didn't wait for an answer but rushed up the stairs.

"An S-O-S text," Slim called after him. Turning to Chad, he said, "You stay down here."

Chad ignored Slim's instructions and followed the three men up the stairs. They made the turn into the kitchen, and Chad saw Dr. Nate run smack into the Shelly woman. She flew backwards across the room and landed on her bottom, the gun going one direction and the plastic case with the coin and letter going in another. Chad cheered.

"Watch her, Earl!" Dr. Nate said.

Earl scooped up the pink gun and pointed it at the imposter. "Nothing would make me happier."

Chad followed the other two men into the living room. Where was everyone? What had she done to them? Chad thought his heart was going to stop right then. His legs felt weak, and he couldn't catch his breath.

"Kate? Where are you?" Dr. Nate shouted. He hurried through the living room. Suddenly, pounding came from down the hallway.

"We're in here. Help! Help! In the office."

Chad's legs collapsed under him. He sat down in the middle of the floor and put his face in his hands. *They are okay. Okay.*

Kate had never been so happy to see someone in her life. When her dad opened the door with the skeleton key from the bedroom door, she threw herself into his arms. He squeezed her so hard it almost took her breath away. She pushed him away. "Dad, that isn't Shelly. I don't know what her name is, but it's not Shelly."

Her dad nodded. "I know. I received a call downstairs from the real Shelly. Right before Chad lit up the whole office screaming about a pink gun."

"You got my text, Slim?" Max asked.

"Your text? It came from Susie's phone." Slim shook his head. "That was the scariest text ever. We were just going into Corleigh's Diner across the street for an early lunch. When I saw those words, 'SOS Shelly not Shelly,' we tore over here. When I told Earl, he freaked. He knows that woman."

"Where is she?" Max asked. "Did she get away?"

"Oh, no. Not a chance."

Kate's dad led the way into the kitchen. The imposter sat on the floor, her head in her hands. Earl leaned against the doorway, gun pointed right at her.

As soon as Earl saw Kate and her dad, he handed the gun to Dr. Nate, who laid it on the counter.

"That's one sweet owl head revolver there," Earl said.

"It was Pinky's," Dr. Nate said. He grinned. "I doubt she ever fired it, but who was to know that? She was one tough granny."

Chad hung on Max's arm. "You should have seen when we came through the door. Dr. Nate ran smack into her, and she flew clear across the room and landed on her bottom."

Earl held his hand out toward the imposter in mock formality. "Let me introduce you to my old high school classmate. Meet Patsy Wells. She was trouble when we were kids: a liar, a cheat, and an opportunist. I thought I recognized her the other day, and when I found the money in my coat, I knew she was the same old Patsy."

Patsy jerked her head up and glared at Earl. "You just had to come and ruin everything, didn't you? It was going so well until you showed up." The words burst out of her with such anger that Kate stepped closer to her dad. "I had to get rid of you before you blew the whole plan, so I took the money. I figured you would run away when you were accused of stealing." She smirked. "You always did run away when trouble came along."

Earl shook his head. "Oh, but I have changed, Patsy, unlike you. I've learned a lot, and one thing I've learned is that running isn't always the answer." He shrugged. "I didn't know that when I got here, but I sure do now."

Kate's dad shook his head. "I'm sorry, man. I wish I had believed you. She sure had me fooled." He pulled Kate close. "Not my daughter, though."

Kate shook her head. "When I saw her leave the Johnson's backyard Wednesday night, I knew something was bad wrong, but I didn't know what to do about it."

"Chad, you saved the day, going downstairs for help like that," Max said, admiration in his voice.

Chad stood taller. "I was scouting outside the door when I heard Aunt Susie say to put down the gun. That shocked me right out of my make-believe world and into the real one." He frowned. "I don't like it when the real world's scarier than make-believe."

"That text was pretty ingenious too, Max," Aunt Susie said. "But my poor phone. It's smashed on the floor in there."

Max grimaced. "I'm sorry, Aunt Susie. I wasn't even sure the text went through before she destroyed it."

"And what about that phone call from the real Shelly?" Her dad put his arm around Kate. "How did you manage that?"

She held out the letter. "We found this the other day, and besides making us think this woman wasn't Shelly, the real Shelly had written down her phone number. I wanted to make sure I wasn't wrong before I told you, so I called it. When I heard her voice on her voice mail, I knew this wasn't Shelly."

"Why didn't you come tell me?" her dad asked.

"That was the plan, Dad." Kate looked at her feet. "I wasn't sure you would believe me without proof, but the other kids made me promise we wouldn't confront her without you. But I got so mad when I knew for sure she was an imposter that I lost it. Carly tried to get me to stop and come down to get you, but I wouldn't." She hung her head. "You know how I get when I'm mad."

Her dad sighed. "I'm sorry. I should have listened to your concerns more closely." He shuddered. "I'm glad you are all okay." He tipped Kate's chin up. "And we must work on that temper of yours."

They heard steps on the stairs. Then two policemen, guns drawn, appeared in the doorway. When they saw the relaxed group, they lowered the weapons. "We got a report of a situation with a gun?"

Nate pointed to the gun, now sitting on the counter. "There's the gun."

Kate stepped forward and pointed to the woman on the floor. "And there is the imposter, thief, and kidnapper."

At 1:30 Saturday afternoon they were all back at the apartment, except Patsy Wells, who had been booked into the jail on several charges including kidnapping and attempted robbery. When the cousins, Carly's parents, Slim, Earl, and Aunt Susie arrived, Kate and her dad were already there. So was Shelly. The real Shelly. Dr. Nate and Kate had picked her up at the airport that morning.

Excited voices and laughter filled the room as Kate introduced Shelly.

Carly couldn't stop smiling at the sight of Kate and Shelly together. *Now that's more like it.* Kate looked at Shelly with unabashed admiration, and Shelly . . . well . . . she reminded Carly so much of Kate's mom that she almost cried. Dr. Nate, too, seemed overwhelmed.

The group settled into spots in the living room, the adults on the furniture and the kids on the floor. Kate sat in front of Shelly and leaned back against her legs.

Shelly shook her head. "I feel terrible this happened. If I had come sooner, if I had listened to my gut and met my best childhood buddy's husband and daughter, no one would have been able to fool them." She looked at her hands. "Kathy always tried to tell me there was more to life than work."

Dr. Nate smiled. "That sounds like Kathy. Well, we're glad you are here now. We're not going to dwell on the shoulda-woulda-couldas, are we?"

Kate shook her head. "Like mom always said, 'Keep looking forward.'"

"Well, I'm looking forward to seeing the necklace," Shelly said.

"You've never seen the necklace in person?" Carly rested her chin on her knees.

"Only once," Shelly said. "One day when we were here, Pinky went into her office and shut the door. We heard banging, and when she came out, she told us the story."

"Tell us," Kate said.

"Well, you know the basic story of how Simon was a close friend of Buffalo Bill, who gave him the necklace and coins the day he got married, along with the letter, right?"

"That letter is what makes it really valuable, isn't it?" Brandon asked.

Shelly nodded. "It sure is. That's what they call the provenance, the proof of the story." She sighed. "That's why Patsy tried to steal it. But what she really wanted was the necklace."

"What's so special about a necklace?" Chad wrinkled up his nose.

Slim smiled at Chad. "I was wondering the same thing, Scout."

Shelly laughed. "Well, it came from the archduke also. Buffalo Bill gave it to Simon before his wedding, for his bride. It's not so much the necklace that's valuable—they're only seed pearls and semi-precious stones—but it's the story that goes with it and its connection to both the Russian archduke and Buffalo Bill."

"Wow!" Chad's eyes sparkled. "So this necklace came from Buffalo Bill?"

"Yep," Shelly said. "And ever since, whenever a girl in our family gets married, she gets to wear the necklace." She squeezed Kate's shoulders. "Kathy was the last one who wore it. And someday, Miss Kate can wear it."

Carly hugged her knees. "What a wonderful story. I sure hope you know where to find it, Miss Shelly. We've looked high and low, and we can't find it anywhere."

Shelly shook her head. "You won't find it unless you know where she put it. Should we go get it?"

"Yes!" Chad jumped to his feet. "I'm ready!"

"I'm not sure you will all enjoy coming with me though," Shelly said.

"Why?" asked Max.

"It's in the office. I think you've had enough experience being crammed in that room?"

Carly felt chills run up her spine again at the thought. "That was a terrible experience."

"Just don't shut the door," Max said.

CHAPTER 15

Buffalo Bill's Russian Jewels

IN THE END IT WAS decided that only Kate, Carly, Dr. Nate, and Shelly would go into the office.

"I don't think we all need to know where the hiding place is anyway," said Carly's dad. "We'll wait out here."

Dr. Nate nodded. "I plan on putting that necklace in a safety deposit box if Shelly won't take it with her."

Shelly laughed. "I think that's the best idea yet. Okay, girls. Let's go."

In the office, Carly watched as Shelly opened the roll top desk. She pulled out a drawer, reached her fingers into it and pushed on the side.

"It has a hidden compartment," Shelly said.

Carly watched her pull her hand out, then she opened it. A small purple velvet bag rested in her palm. There it was. Carly shivered with excitement. They had found the treasure.

"Let's go back in the living room so the others can see," Shelly said.

Once there, Shelly opened the pouch and laid the necklace on the coffee table. The gold chain was dainty and perfect. The natural pearls shone, and the sparkly stones around the pearls looked like diamonds. It was the most beautiful piece of jewelry Carly had ever seen. A hush came over the room. Even Chad stared at the necklace, his eyes wide.

"Whoa!" Chad said.

"There you are. The family treasure, Buffalo Bill's Russian jewels," Shelly said. "Feel how soft this little bag is." She handed it to Kate, who rubbed the velvet and then handed it to Carly.

"I remember when Kathy wore it," Dr. Nate said. He stroked Kate's hair. "Your mother was so worked up, I teased her that she was more excited about wearing the necklace than she was about marrying me." He turned to the others. "I don't know how we'll ever thank you for helping clean out all Pinky's stuff," Dr. Nate said. He looked around the room. "I've met a lot of people in my day, but you folks, you are top-notch. Look at this place—it's almost empty!"

"And the best part is that they helped get rid of the worst trash," Kate said.

"What's that?" her dad asked.

"The fake Shelly," Kate said. "I'll be glad if I never see her again."

Shelly sighed. "I'm going over to the jail later today to talk to her. We've known each other a lot of years, and she was a good caregiver for Mom. I am not happy about what she has done, but I still feel like I should reach out to her and see if she's at all willing to let me help."

Max shook his head. "She sounded kind of like she didn't much like you."

Aunt Susie reached out and touched Shelly's arm. "I'll go with you. You're right. She needs help."

Earl looked around the room and then leaned forward. "Dr. Nate, if this apartment weren't so pink, it wouldn't be half bad. Slim and I have been talking about finding an apartment we could rent together since I think I'll stay awhile. Could we make a deal on the deposit if we do the painting?"

Dr. Nate's eyes crinkled with a smile. "That would be awesome."

Slim grinned. "We can eat breakfast over at Corleigh's every day if we want. I've become kind of addicted to those sandwiches they call 'Muh Nick.'"

Carly's dad's phone rang. He pulled it out of his pocket and looked at the number. "It's your brother," he said to his wife, holding the phone out to her.

She shook her head. "Oh no, you don't," she said. "It's your sister. *You* talk to them."

Carly giggled.

"What's going on?" Kate asked.

"We couldn't get a hold of our parents last night after the incident," Max explained. "They were at the competition until late, then back there again this morning. We didn't want to leave that kind of news on a voice mail, so they don't know yet." He grinned at his aunt and uncle. "Neither of them wants to tell my parents what happened." Carly's dad finally answered. "Hi, Jack, just a minute," he said. "Max wants to talk to you." He handed the phone to Max. "Here, Detective Rawson. You do the *'splaining.*"

Others In This Series:

The Double Cousins and the Mystery of the Missing Watch

The Double Cousins and the Mystery of the Torn Map

The Double Cousins and the Mystery of the Rushmore Treasure

The Double Cousins and the Mystery of Custer's Gold

Also by Miriam Jones Bradley:

The Nearly Twins and the Secret in the Mason Jar

All I Have Needed—A Legacy for Life

You Ain't From Here, Are Ya? Reflections on Southern Culture from an Outsider

If you enjoyed this book and
would like to read more by

MIRIAM JONES BRADLEY

please visit:

www.MiriamJonesBradley.com
miriamjonesbradley@gmail.com
@AuthorMiriam
www.facebook.com/DoubleCousinsMysteries

For more information about
AMBASSADOR INTERNATIONAL
please visit:

www.ambassador-international.com
@AmbassadorIntl
www.facebook.com/AmbassadorIntl